FINDING TAKRI

Palo Stickland

FINDING TAKRI

Palo Stickland

First published 2013 by Dahlia Publishing Ltd
6 Samphire Close Hamilton
Leicester LE5 1RW
ISBN 9780956696748

Printed and bound by Berforts

To my foster-Grandmother Jenna

Still hoping you arrived safe
Rest in Peace

PART ONE

CHAPTER ONE

Glasgow 2005

My Grandmother Takri was the only person who remembered the date I was born.

'She said it was the fifteenth of the Punjabi month of Chet,' my mother told me. 'It was your father who was wrong.'

I discovered that Chet followed the lunar year and calculated that my birthday must be in March. Sadly, by the time I was able to do this, I had acquired another birth date, one my father was forced to produce at speed, in answer to a demand by a headmistress, when I was registered at her school in Glasgow. He chose the second of January and that became my birthday. In the absence of a birth certificate, neither of them checked my passport, where the year was also different from the one my father gave. I discarded the one used at school when I left, and became a year older over the space of a summer holiday.

Birthdays had no importance in my family when I was young. They were the last festivals adopted by us in our new country. Christmas was the first, and became the most important, when the children received gifts: and Easter, when chocolate eggs were bought but only for the youngest. Though new customs continued to infiltrate our lives as, in my thirties, my parents began visiting on my birthday and having the usual discussion/argument over a cup of tea and cake.

'It's your father's fault. He forgot and doesn't want to admit it,' my mother would glare at him. He would ignore her, pretending to be engrossed in conversation with my husband.

Then, on one occasion, attempting to help him, I asked, 'Why did you choose January, Papa?'

'Isn't it obvious? I wanted you to start in the first class, to make it easier for you at school.'

'And you decided I could be a year younger?'

'No, no. That was your mother's doing. I remember it well - the day I left the village you were a walking baby. You were not one year old yet, and that was in December 1949. So I was right.' He would breathe deeply and square up his shoulders to emphasise the point. It happened every year.

'He doesn't remember,' my mother would whisper to me. In our community, we cannot apologise gracefully. This was their way of saying sorry to me.

Whoever was to blame, as a girl with a disputed birthday, I was extremely annoyed; it seemed that everyone had their special day but me. My brother's was not forgotten, and I managed to find an explanation for that, in the sixties, when I had returned to the Punjab. My youngest brother was minutes old, and when I entered the room where my mother lay with the baby, and told me it was important to remember the exact time of his birth, in order that his horoscope could be drawn up. I looked at the clock and memorised that it was 11.17pm on 17th February 1962.

But for girls it was quite different. 'What a pity, it's a girl,' was the usual comment, and the family would be downcast, thinking of nothing but the financial expense to come at her wedding: so no forecast of the future was required. Although on my birth, my grandmother insisted no-one should have a long face. Again, according to my mother, Takri's words were, 'she is not a burden because her brother needs a sister.' And then she named me after *him*, as was the custom in those days. By the time I was old enough to question this, to express my displeasure, everyone thought it was cute; a connection, rather like being a twin. When I was young I always thought my name was a particularly masculine one, perhaps only because it was my brother's, hated it and called myself Rupa. I did ask myself why my grandmother had given me that name. Was it that she cared so little, and only lumbered me with my brother's name for convenience?

It was many years before I would find out that my grandmother adored me. She was an accomplished woman who was not daunted by having to live in a male dominated world and by naming me after my brother she was making the statement that I was as good as he was.

At times of transition in my life, I have believed that from somewhere in those early years my grandmother continues to send that message to me. When confused about the behaviour of father, mother, brother or husband I would search for answers in my mind and it was her voice that I always heard, 'This is the way it is, but you are strong and will prevail. You are equal to anyone.'

I don't remember leaving her when I was five, but I do know that in the first few years of living in Glasgow, I was extremely unhappy. She, who had been a buffer and a solace, in my often troubled relationships with my unhappy mother and volatile brother, had slipped from my life. Blue airmail letters arrived from my uncle, but Takri had never been to school, learned a little Punjabi at home but with little use the knowledge had gone. If I was ever mentioned, I was not told: certainly no

11

phone calls came from the happy, sunny place left behind. Here, there were only cold February pavements and grey stone tenements.

My one consolation was Baba Kam who came to live, with Betty, in the flat below ours in Grafton Square. My parents approved of him as he came from the same area in the Punjab so I was allowed to spend time with them. I adopted them as grandparents and remember running from school to show them my prize book, the first anyone in my family owned. Betty bought me my first possession, a bright red purse with a gold clasp. Baba Kam took me to the Indian cinema on Sundays until the day I told him, in English, that I didn't understand the language spoken in the film but behind my decision to say this was my mother's frowning at my going, as she said I was too old now. It was the initial crack in the rift between us: so many bans without explanation.

'Don't go near boys. You're a woman now,' she said when I felt like a vunerable child at beginning my periods aged twelve.

Baba Kam had time to sit with me and listen and answer questions in his deep voice with only a hint of an Indian accent. He told me he'd come to Glasgow before the war and that was so long ago.

But I couldn't ask Baba what to do when a boy persistently approached me. Late one winter afternoon I was sent out on an errand. It had already grown dark and the light in the close was on. I was near the close mouth when the boy, three years my senior, came up from behind and pinned me to the wall with his body. I was afraid as he pushed his hand down my blouse to grab my breast. I pushed, but then there were steps from the street, and Baba appeared and saw my frightened face.

With a yell, he pulled the boy away, lifting him off his feet. I had never seen Baba angry: he was like a lion that lies so quiet but can leap and roar when provoked. I slid to the floor bursting into tears while he shouted abuse at the boy who disappeared back up the stairs to his flat.

Baba said, 'Hush, it's over now.' He lifted me up and hugged me. I was so much stronger after this incident: it was as if some of the lion's strength had crossed over to me.

Years later I learned of the link between Baba Kam and my grandmother and wondered if Baba was kind to me only because of her.

A lifetime has passed.

I wish I could tell them that I understand what they passed down to me, and that they succeeded in making me brave; if only now, I could find the link between them.

I would need the help of my parents and last year, as I held my new-born nephew I thought of his loss. He will not know Takri who lived through tumultuous times in India; perhaps not even remember his own grandmother, my mother, now in her eighties. And that is how I approached my parents. Tell me and I will record the past for your grandchildren.

I still had doubts. Was it possible to discover the story of my grandparents and have enough information to write about their lives? Was I up to such a task? I wondered.

First, I learned to question my parents with care, and then to think behind those answers, at what was not being said; the feelings that they hid intentionally, the facts they considered unimportant, but that I needed to build the whole picture. And my own memories must be included.

The Search Begins

My mother sighed when she finally agreed that I could write Takri's story, 'There was much sorrow in her life. Sometimes I would catch her looking into the distance as she sat sewing, or at her spinning wheel, with a look so sad. She was married young, but that was the custom.'

We are in her Glasgow suburban living room; a Wimpey house named after the building company that raised whole estates of affordable homes. A small room with space only for a sofa, two armchairs and a television but personalised with the huge graduation photos in ornate frames that look down on us from the walls. The oldest is mine, and then my younger brothers, my son and my nieces. My older brother has no photo in this gallery and now I believe he has suffered from Asperger's syndrome, but was never diagnosed, so his achievements are different.

My mother's voice brings me back to the present, to her memories, 'Girls could have a wedding as a seven-year-old but it wasn't consummated; you visited your in-laws after the ceremony and then returned to your home. When you were older, your parents sent you off with more gifts, you know I've always said, having a girl is being the giver of gifts; and that second time was when you met your husband. My mother Takri was sent to live with her in-laws because my cousin was orphaned.'

'Your cousin?'

'Yes. Her parents were Takri's sister and her husband, only teenagers at the time when they succumbed to the plague.'

Plague? The only one I knew was from Scottish history lessons – the Great Plague of London, 1665 - so I thought she was mistaken about a feared, horrific disease from three centuries in the past. To find it was true that the bubonic plague was still a threat to life in India, and in the land-locked Punjab, in the twentieth century, came as a shock

'And what about Baba Kam? Did Grandmother know him then?' I knew the answer but I wanted her memory.

'We haven't spoken of him since he left. He was close to you. Do you remember? He told me when he came to India that they had been friends in Delhi, and Kam, he was actually called Karam but changed his name when he fled India. He was a freedom-fighter against the British Raj, did you know, Rupa?'

I nodded and looked away. I knew more than my mother Saira did, but I couldn't tell her. It was long ago and I have many memories though sometimes I think I dreamed them. But I remember Karam Singh, who became my Baba Kam; Basant Singh, my grandfather and Takri who loved them both.

CHAPTER TWO

Rurka 1956

In the courtyard of Basant's house, the following year, on a fine spring morning, Durgee joined Takri under the shade of the veranda, when their chores were done. Takri sat on a low stool, behind her spinning wheel beside a pile of pencil-thin rolls of fine, white cotton wool. Taking each one in her right hand, and spinning the wheel with her left she pulled a thin, steady line of thread run from the sharp end of the spindle. Each line was piled onto the middle of the spindle, and then she pulled the wool up again.

'You must miss Saira, especially now she has a new baby,' said Durgee, who frowned in concentration on her knitting: it was a difficult design, with two colours of wool.

'I wish they were here. Jaspal and Rupa were born in our front room, but this little boy is so far away. We don't know when we'll see him. They're together as a family though, that's what matters.'

'How is this baby's colouring? Has she mentioned it, at all?'

'Tut,' prickled Takri, 'Skin colour, again. Whatever the problem with her father's and then with Saira's skin, it's not being passed down to her children.'

'That awful woman at the end of the street calls you 'the albino family' because of Basant's skin, but everyone knows she's a troublesome witch.'

'The poor soul certainly has problems,' answered Takri closing the topic.

They continued in silence until they heard the click, click of a walking stick running along the walls in the lane.

'It's lunchtime already, and that's your husband come home for lunch. I'll be off then,' the neighbour picked up her wool and was out of the door before Basant and his helper came in.

Not quick enough for Basant's hearing, 'Is that you Durgee? You don't have to leave because I'm here,' he called.

'I'm going to prepare lunch for my son. How could I have thought, I could slip past you?' Durgee laughed.

Basant stepped carefully click-clicking into the courtyard with Sunny, his helper.

'Sit here, uncle,' the boy pulled over a mat, taking Basant's stick from him.

'Thank you, little one,' said Basant. 'You're a great support to me Sunny.'

Takri placed a tray of chapattis and vegetables in front of Basant. The boy brought a tumbler of water, and putting it beside the tray said, 'Uncle, I've put the water here.' He took Basant's hand and placed it over the tumbler. Basant nodded.

'Have you been to the old workshop, this morning?' Takri asked the boy.

'Yes, Aunt. First, after breakfast, I took Uncle to the nearly built workshop on the main road. The joiner is fitting windows there. Then, I came back to the old workshop in the bazaar where the work is going on. I made some deliveries, and then, I went back to the new workshop to bring Uncle for lunch,' he smiled.

'After all that, you deserve your food. Here you are.'

'I could go between the new and old workshops alone if it were not for the open space between the village and the road,' said Basant.

'It's safer to have someone with you,' Takri declared, 'and Sunny enjoys helping you. I can tell. As well as that his mother needs the money we pay him. Remember when our boys started work when they were young?'

'Yes. Our sons have worked hard.'

Sunny added, 'That new road is busy, so I should always be with you, Uncle. And Aunt, do you know what the talk in the bazaar is today?'

'No, tell me Sunny.'

The child's face lit up, 'It's all about freedom fighters. They've to receive pensions from the government. It's because they helped free India from the British.'

'That's good,' and Takri's thoughts shot into the past. Delhi ... Calcutta ... Amritsar.

'Did you know any freedom fighters, Uncle?' Sunny continued.

'Oh yes. I had a good friend who was always disappearing off to cause problems for the British. I often wonder what happened to him.'

The boy noticed the tears in Takri's eyes.

'Did he die? Then there's no pension for him.'

'Many heroes disappeared, Sunny. And those who are still alive deserve their pensions.'

'Yes, Uncle. Perhaps we should go now,' Sunny noticing Takri's sad face, helped clear the dishes before bringing water to let Basant wash his hands. Takri wiped away a tear.

'I'm sorry, Aunt,' he whispered. 'That freedom fighter was your friend too?'

'Sort of,' she answered and started on cleaning the dishes in the wet corner.

'See you later, Aunt.'

The boy and the blind man set out through the bazaar to the new workshop near the crossroads. Sunny, busy checking the path for large stones, did not notice the tall, grey-haired stranger watching them cross the open land in front of the cluster of village houses.

Karam felt a physical pain, and sighed deeply, as the man and boy came into view from the shadowy lane between the box-like, flat-roofed houses of Rurka. The man gave an impression of all-whiteness. His turban was white, as was his face and beard and his long shirt and pyjama-trousers were white. His shoes were brown and dusty. Karam knew his eyes would be pink, his eyelashes and eyebrows white.

Basant touched his stick rhythmically along the ground, taking careful steps, with his left hand on Sunny's shoulder. The boy was his eyes along this stretch to the new workshop.

As the pair crossed the road, letting the dust which blew up on the passing of the brightly painted truck settled, and the stranger in the long dark blue coat moved out of the shade, and walked along to the gate, and entered behind them.

It was a large space of about fifteen yards square, with a seven foot high perimeter wall. Two rooms had been built to the left hand side, verandas shading the doorways. Two mature trees, a mango and a neem gave shade in the far left hand corner where the joiner was sawing wood for the window frames. There was a room at the far end to the right, with a hand-pump in front of it, facing the gate. Near the pump, against the wall was a small open fireplace. There was a string-bed in the sun near the veranda.

'Sit on the string-bed, Uncle. I'll bring a glass of water from the pump.'

'Good. Is that a saw, I hear?'

'Yes, Uncle. The joiner is here, making the windows.'

'Have you had lunch, son?' Basant called to the joiner.

'Yes, sir, I have,' the young man answered.

'Who is there? Someone at the gate? I may be blind but my hearing is good.'

'Ahem,' Karam cleared his throat, 'Ah ... I've come from Mehatpur, friend.'

'Sat siri akal ji,' Sunny folded his hands to the stranger.

'What does the visitor look like, Sunny. You understand, friend, Sunny is my eyes.'

'He is very tall, Uncle. He has grey hair and light brown eyes, very light.'

'I used to have a good friend from Mehatpur, Sunny,' Basant stood up, 'He had sparkling eyes and a merry voice. He was a freedom fighter. We remembered him this morning, didn't we?'

'You said he must have died.' Sunny's eyes were glued to the visitor's face and he felt afraid. The man was old but tall, straight and there was power, his body looked ready to pounce, but the strength was also in his eyes. Sunny couldn't resist the visitor's gaze.

'Friend, I might know you if I touched your face. Will you let me?'

'I had thought, perhaps my voice would ...' Karam began.

'Karam? Come here ... Karam Singh!' Basant stumbled forward into Karam's arms.

While the two friends laughed and cried, Sunny ran for water. The joiner had stopped work. Seeing the two men embrace in tears he stopped the boy from disturbing them.

'Why ... did you stay away? It's been years since Independence.'

'I ... thought you wouldn't want to see me.'

'Oh? After Amritsar? I ran away and joined Gandhi. You disappeared. Takri was here, the strongest of us. We were all young and India was changing: we were changing. It's all in the past now. Let me feel your face, Karam. No beard? No turban? A proper Englishman! I wouldn't have known you, even if I'd had my eyes. Still thin, you always came back starving. Remember, you remember! From those exploits, those freedom-fighter escapades. Sunny, bring water.'

'Come, sir,' the joiner interrupted, walking forward to shake hands with Karam, 'I'll pump the water for you to wash. We'll brew tea. It seems there should be a celebration. You haven't met since Jallianwala? Nearly forty years! I wasn't born yet.'

'I'll run to the house and bring sugar and milk. Will you be alright, Uncle?'

'I've never been in better hands, my boy. Karam is here. Tell Aunt, but tell her quietly, so she doesn't feel a shock.'

'She cried this morning but I'll not let her cry now.'

'Let's both wash at the pump, Karam. Don't want the lady in our lives to see our tears. Help me, my friend.'

Sunny raced across the road, over the open space to the houses, through the miller's lane to the bazaar and into the lane, as someone rang the temple bell, and into Takri's courtyard. He was out of breath and sat down on the doorstep from where he could see her spinning.

'Sunny?'

'Yes ... Aunt ... everything ... is alright. I have good news.'

'You shouldn't have run. Come in and have a drink of water, then tell me.'

Sunny began before he got to the water-jar, 'Aunt, you remember we were talking about freedom-fighters this morning? And you won't cry. Promise me first.'

'If you ask me not to cry, I'll make myself so strong, I won't. What's happened?'

'There is a visitor at the workshop and I came back for milk and sugar. Can we have some white sugar not the brown lumps?'

'This is a special visitor, if you want our rationed sugar,' Takri was amused at the boy's enthusiasm but continued her spinning.

'And you have to come too. They are waiting.'

'I haven't been to the workshop since the foundation stone was laid. Sunny, who is it?'

But Sunny had run inside, 'I'll get your outdoor skirt.'

'Sunny, answer my question.'

'It is our freedom-fighter, Aunt. It's Karam Singh. They cried. You should have seen them hug each other,' Sunny willed that Takri wouldn't cry but, 'Aunt ... don't ...'

Takri's hands had let go the spinning wheel and flown to her face. Her eyes wide and brimming but it was Sunny who burst into tears and her arms opened for him. They held each other, hearts beating in unison, then the beat escaped and was in their heads and their arms until their breathing regained its normal calm. The child's tears wet Takri's shoulder, she let him go and he sat in front of her on the ground. She pushed away her spinning wheel and rose to lift her outdoor skirt which he'd brought to her.

'I'm not crying, Sunny, but you've had too much emotion for a morning. Go and splash water on your face and I'll get the milk and sugar. Don't rub your eyes.'

'Yes, Aunt. No, I won't.' He scrambled to the wet corner.

They walked in silence back through the lane. Several people looked with interest; Takri's son stopped turning bolts on his lathe in the workshop in the main street, but on seeing the purposeful gait of his mother, in her black outdoor skirt and dupatta, with the boy skipping by her side, he returned to his task.

At the gate of the new workshop, she stopped to raise her veil with one hand, sighed deeply as she stepped over the threshold.

In front of the veranda of the two rooms to her left there were two string beds on one Basant sat leaning over as if he was looking at his feet. As he heard the swishing of her long skirt and her footsteps at the gate he stood up, raising his hand as if to quieten her. She had made no noise: now her gaze fell on the other bed where a figure lay sleeping: it's only resemblance to Karam was the length and girth, there was no turban she noticed. She leaned over and Sunny pushed towards her, afraid she might fall. He gripped her hand tighter until she looked down at him.

'I'm fine, dear,' she whispered.

23

She moved towards the far end of the courtyard, to the fire and the room behind it, where she removed the heavy outdoor skirt that tradition demanded she wear over her salwar-kameez, outside of her home. She felt tired of it, and vowed to discard it today. Karam had cut his hair, why shouldn't she change too. She hung the skirt on a hook, and sat down to brew the tea. The joiner, who was smoothing wood for the window-frames, gave her a nod and a smile, to let her know he'd heated the water.

Sunny had collected five smooth stones and was playing a game under the mango tree, leaving Takri to return to her thoughts. She could hardly believe she was brewing tea for Karam and Basant. Often, especially in the years following Independence and the partition of the Punjab she would run the past over in her mind and try to imagine Karam's return, how it might be. Would he walk into her courtyard in the lane? Would she meet him on the street, on the train? How would Basant behave? And now, it was happening. All the years between had fallen away like leaves from the trees in autumn – and she felt forty years younger. She had poured the tea into the clay tumblers when she glanced over and her eyes met Karam's. He lay as she had first seen him on entering the courtyard, only his eyes were open. And they were his green-brown eyes and that look that had haunted her dreams for the years of separation. One long look, and then she slid her veil down over her forehead, to cover the eyes that would surely give her away, that would affect her speaking voice so Basant would hear, or bring tears that the joiner might misinterpret, better to hide them as always.

She began pouring the tea: the joiner came over to distribute the tumblers. She rose from the mat where she had sat cross-legged in front of the fire, aware that Karam was rising from the bed and approaching her.

'Sat siri akal,' he looked into her eyes, the veil was very thin, the joiner and Sunny were behind him fussing around Basant.

'Sat siri akal ... you look different, but well,' she managed to say.

'I've been in England since 1930. A place to the north of England,' he moved back to his place on the bed. Takri sat down beside Basant.

'When did you return?' asked Basant and then raising his voice, 'No. First drink. Drink your tea, Karam. Sunny, did you give your Aunt a shock?'

'He was very careful. I used to wonder if you'd just walk into the house one day, Karam, but it's been eight years since Independence, so we believed the worst.'

'I asked the Congress-wale in the village to let me know if there was news of you,' Basant added.

'I fled because I was wanted by the law in India. England was the safest place.'

'You mean, in the home of the rulers. That was a clever move,' said the joiner.

'There were dissidents there too. You know of Udham Singh?

'Didn't he avenge the massacre by killing the governor?' the joiner asked.

'I was with him the day before he shot O'Dwyer, and then I went to Scotland.'

Takri watched the three men talk, wondering how she would find the time and place to speak to Karam on her own. It seemed impossible, her daughters-in-law had both gone to a

25

wedding this week but on their return – well, perhaps she could spend a day in Mehatpur – or send a message. Did he have a family? What about the daughter, his daughter who she had given away? She heard him tease the boy and ask if he was their grandson.

'No, I work for Uncle,' stated Sunny proudly.

'His father died two years ago,' Takri began.

'He takes care of me,' explained Basant. 'That's his job, and he earns three rupees a day and gives them to his mother.'

'We have two sons and a daughter, Karam. What about you?' Takri had to know to work out what she must tell him.

'I never married.'

Takri looked away towards the fire, to hide her shock, and said, 'I should go to the house now. Seeing you, I've come to a decision about that heavy skirt I wear outdoors.'

'Oh, what are you going to do?' asked Sunny.

'There was such a change forty years ago. We all gathered in the maidan and burnt our foreign cloth, Sunny.'

'Our freedom fighters shaved their heads and beards,' added Basant.

'That's right,' laughed Karam.

'And now I am going to shed that heavy skirt. Times are changing and women shouldn't need to cover over their normal salwar-kameez. I'm going to walk through the bazaar without it. Sunny you can take it to your mother but tell her, I said she doesn't have to wear it. She can use the material.'

'Yes Aunt.'

'About time too,' agreed Basant. 'If we make the decision the younger ones will follow. Will you stay with us, Karam?' Basant asked, 'then you can meet the boys. And stay as long as you like. You always came back to me? Remember?'

26

'I did. But I told my nephews I would be back tonight. I'll visit for a longer time another day. This is enough excitement for today, eh Sunny?'

CHAPTER THREE

Punjab to Delhi

The train sped through lush green fields broken in the distance by lines of tall trees which shaded the roads. It was the daily express from Amritsar to Delhi.

Karam's eyes were on the fields rolling past the barred window, but he did not see them. Alone at last, he wanted to remember each detail of the last week to help him understand the change in his life. He'd come to India to re-connect with his nephews and Basant; to find Takri again hoping his actions had not caused too much damage. How could he have been so naive, so uncaring of what would happen to her after their love-making? What excuse could he have? Hadn't he been a rash, selfish man with a cruel, one-track mind – only that it was a lifetime ago and that time was another world. And how could he make amends? His action had produced a daughter who was now, if still living, a prostitute – his daughter, his beautiful Jat girl – he imagined how it could have been – his mother preparing a lunch, lifting the basket to the head of his tall, slim, smiling daughter, sending her out to her brother who tended his crops in their green, Punjabi fields. Why did he not see that vision, that right order of country living, when he was young? He'd seen India being taken by the British, first for themselves, and wanted to change that. The young Karam had decided freedom was the future.

And now, old Karam, foolish Karam, who has hidden in the enemy camp all these years, fate has dealt you a blow. You thought India would be a new and wonderful country. In this new India your daughter, who should have been a proud girl with her own fields, taking meals to a husband and sons, lives by selling her body in Delhi.

He had been physically sick when Takri told him. And only when she said, 'Perhaps, she managed to escape the worst of our fears. She's not from the community that brought her up, she's a Punjabi. She'll be strong.'

'I'll find her.'

'In the city?'

'The red-light area is not so large.'

'Red, the colour of blood, there are words engraved on my heart, it seems, in that colour. Nur, daughter of Sajida Begum, House One, Babur Chowk, The Friday Mosque Road, Old Delhi,' Takri let out a sob that seemed to have been caught in her body since decades. Her head fell towards her lap.

'Sajida ... she was well-known in the Delhi of my youth,' murmured Karam.

'You knew her! Oh God.'

'What age is our daughter now?'

'Our daughter? She'll be in her thirties. Five years older than Saira. Thirty-six. Don't condemn her, Karam, it wasn't her fault.'

'No, the fault was mine.'

'And mine. Both of us.'

The train pulled in to Delhi station, and Karam prepared to weave his way through the river of humanity that always filled it. As he alighted, a coolie in a red shirt came forward to take his

29

brown leather case. Karam nodded, and watched as the man, thin wiry and very strong, crouched, adjusted the cloth wrapped around his head, lifted and placed the case on it and stretched to his full six-foot height. He moved easily through the crowd, and Karam followed sometimes falling behind but able to see the suitcase above the crowd. The coolie stopped at the rickshaw stand, and waited for his tip. Karam paid, and on hearing double the usual price to his hotel near Chandni Chowk, two rupees, raised his eyebrows answered, 'one-only, one rupee' and prepared to move to another rickshaw. The man shrugged in agreement, stepping in front of Karam to lift his suitcase to the back.

At the hotel, Karam washed and set out in the evening for a meal at a local eatery, a dhaba, which was a shop front with kitchen at the front and seats, either chairs or benches with tables, at the back. Large pots of dal and vegetable curry simmered over fires at the entrance, for potential customers to view, the smell of the food wafting out to pedestrians. The proprietor, the usual plump, cheerful character sitting cross-legged at the side of the entrance, enticed customers with a smile as his hands shaped the naan breads to be placed in the oven at his side.

'Ah sir, fresh naan breads and dal for you. Come on in. You are welcome.'

As Karam ate, the naan and dal with cream floating on top was delicious, he decided he would change his original plan and head for the red-light district that evening. He wouldn't be able to speak to anyone for the evening was the courtesans' time to entertain with music and dance, but he could make himself acquainted with the place.

30

Paying the cheerful, chubby proprietor he left with the words ringing in his ears, 'See you tomorrow, sir. Welcome in the morning for breakfast also.'

The thirty years or so he had spent in England and Scotland gave him away, his clothes and manner marked him as a 'foreign-returned'; a customer with money. And now to the red-light area: in his younger days he had skipped and laughed his way along these streets. Today he wished he was a thousand miles from here. Leaving the rickshaw about a mile from his destination, he walked in front of the steps of the Friday Mosque, stopping half-way to look up. About thirty steps led to the massive entrance gate, an ornately carved arch surrounded by Qur'anic verses; he could see two minarets piercing the navy blue evening sky, a crescent moon visible near the exquisite dome. He stood with his eyes on it and prayed in his own way; a prayer for his daughter. Bending, he touched the lowest step of the grand old mosque and lifted his hand to his forehead. Men who were entering or leaving glanced his way, continuing on their own religious business: he turned and strode to the end of the long, winding street, leaving the mosque, and all it stood for, far behind in the gathering dusk.

The shops alongside were open, girls walked along bumping into men to attract their attention, these were common prostitutes, and in the lane there was brightly coloured bunting with red electric lights spanning the five metre wide entrance. As he passed under the lights he glanced on either side of him at the low windows where sparingly clad women sat and beckoned to the stream of men entering and leaving. These were older women, past their prime and left to fend for themselves against abusive and violent clients, whereas the young ones will be dressed in silks, precious jewels and anklet bells in the dancing rooms protected by their madams, their eunochs and others in their community. The women in the windows were the dancing girls of his youth, about twenty on either side; he did not look closely for fear of recognising a face. No, he was sure he wouldn't remember the faces, only Sajida's, but then every man of his generation remembered her, if only for her dancing: to have sex with her had cost a fortune. He'd known men who boasted that they had done, but he'd known they'd lied. If you could afford the most beautiful and accomplished courtesan you couldn't afford to boast about it; you would want to protect your good name and respectability for, ultimately, she was only a prostitute. There was a code of conduct regarding the square at the end of the lane; the men who came here to be entertained regularly, spent fortunes here, did not speak of it outside and were never identified.

I was a little fish in this sea of sharks, Karam thought, and I must not think like a bitter old man, he berated himself, intelligent and benign dolphins also swim in this sea. He came through the lane of red-light windows to a square, a dead end with seven houses of two or three stories, open verandas at every level, where light, music, laughter and perfume wafted into the air around him. And that inky blue sky covers this world too and there's the moon, lit up for all. His gaze fell towards the house at his left hand, a pink-walled three storey mansion; he turned towards it. The animals, carriages and servants would be housed on the ground floor, above that, the women's bedrooms and on the top floor were the dancing rooms. You could join the crowd in the main hall or, with the requisite amount of money have a dance recital on your own. Sex was always extra.
He was stopped at the gate by a burly man.

'How can we help you tonight, sir?' he leaned over and whispered. 'Any special preference?'

'Tonight I wish only to be entertained in the dancing hall.'

'Ah, that will be five rupees and you pay at the top. If you wish anything else my family upstairs can help.'

'Thank you. It was a long time ago that I was here last. There was a dancer called Sajida. You may be too young to remember her,' Karam observed the eunuch's reaction.

'I cannot answer your question, sir. In the morning the madam would be pleased to receive you, if you leave your name with my family.'

'I thought you might say that,' murmured Karam as he stepped past the man before a group of young men, excited and nervous at their naughtiness in being there, approached the gate behind him and pushed past him to the stairs.

'Sorry, uncle,' one of them turned to say, as he brushed past.

Karam stopped to take a breather at the doors on the first landing, then proceeded towards the music and lights of the top floor. He paid the man at the table in front of the dancing hall. At the door another big man, eunuchs tended to put on weight, took him to a spot on the floor where there was a gold-tasselled green bolster. Karam was glad to take off his jacket and lower himself to the floor where he arranged himself in a cross-legged position with an elbow leaning on the fat round cushion. There were reflections of light everywhere from the glass chandeliers, to stars on the walls, to the mirrored embroidery on the clothes of the women and the musicians. He looked around at the room, it was the same size as he remembered, seating forty men easily on one half of the floor, the other half was the 'stage'. There were two principal dancers, late twenties, Karam thought, who also sang and four supporting girl dancers, with three musicians who sat on one of two dais. The other was for the dancers and their madam. The madam looked late forties in age, resplendent in lilac and silver, with silver bangles, earrings, heavy necklace, hair jewellery displayed on the side of her head not covered by her silver-trimmed dupatta. Her eyes were sharp, intelligent and business-like watching the audience for information to use in future negotiations.

Karam thought she was a typical madam, on my last visit here I had no eyes for the madam at all but now I see she is the brains behind the establishment. He expected the position of madam to have been Sajida's by now. He would ask for an interview with this madam whose gaze returned to meet his every time she surveyed the audience.

He enjoyed the music and the lyrics were not too bad. He'd found them quite mediocre in the past, he thought, we used to make jokes of them, but these are clever. The images from the music conveyed him from the hall to starry skies, sailing boats and lands across the seas. During the interval he had approached the desk to request an appointment with the madam. As he returned to his place the madam acknowledged him with a nod, by which he presumed that his interview would indeed take place the next morning. The entertainment resumed, but before he knew it, the midnight hour had passed, and the hall was almost empty. Past midnight was an extra payment. Suddenly the tiredness from his travelling caught up with him and he decided to leave. At the desk, the man said, 'Eleven-thirty tomorrow morning, sir.' He gave a nod, and left.

The morning was cloudy and dull. Karam took a taxi to the Babur Chowk alighting at the entrance to the lane. The same man was at the gate to the first house: this time he accompanied Karam up the stairs. One door on the first landing was open, there was a stairway behind it, probably to the first floor and the rooftop, thought Karam. The smell of washing was in the air not the perfume of the previous evening. He could hear the voices of girls, gossiping and giggling.

On the top landing the doors to the hall were closed and behind the desk, there sat an old woman, small grey-haired, wearing a grey salwar-kameez and dupatta. She gave the man a nod which was the sign for him to return to the gate and then she stood and had a good look at Karam who was looking very distinguished in a grey suit made-to-measure for him in Glasgow. Then she sighed leaving him wondering at her thoughts, but without speaking a word she motioned to him to follow her through the door opposite the dancing hall which led into a room about five metres square. In one corner was a raised dais on which sat the madam whose name was Nargis Akhter, this he'd learned the night before.

Karam removed his shoes and placed them outside the door. Nargis waved an arm towards an array of bolsters and cushions in the middle of the carpeted floor. He removed his jacket and sat down crossing his legs. The corner behind Nargis was curtained and he guessed there were open windows there. A breeze blew the soft, white material into the room.

'Will you have tea, Karam Singh,' her voice was clear and beautiful and he wondered why she hadn't sung the previous night.

'Thank you for offering, Nargis ji, but I had some not half-an-hour ago,' he replied.

35

'How may I be of service to you?' she smiled sweetly with the tiniest hint of innuendo.

'I've returned to Delhi after many years.'

'You have obviously prospered,' she looked him up and down, raising her immaculate eyebrows.

'In a small way but I remembered this establishment from years past.'

'How kind of you to remember us,' she nodded, smiling encouragement.

'I was wondering what happened to Sajida.'

'Ah, she was the courtesan of your youth.'

'Yes, very well renowned and much loved.'

'She died. A weak heart. It must be ten – fifteen years.' She noted the disappointment in his face.

'Are you ... her sister?'

'We're all family here. But no, not a sister though my mother was Sajida's old madam, perhaps from your day.'

'I can't remember. I'm afraid I only had eyes for Sajida,' he noticed the flicker of jealousy on the woman's face, he'd said too much.

She recovered quickly, 'Of course. Each generation to their own.'

'Could you tell me about Sajida's family?'

'Family?'

'Her children?'

'We're very careful whose children we have. You think ...'

'Not in that way. I was not always wealthy and could only afford to watch her dance. I wondered if she had chosen to have a child at all.'

'She had boys.'

'Nur?' As he said the name her icy look told Karam he'd lost the game. She would answer in the negative.

'No. There was no daughter of Sajida's called Nur.'

'Any daughter?'

'It was her misfortune to give birth to three sons. In our community we prefer daughters and hers would have been a prize for this house, I'm sure you'll agree. One of the sons works in House number three. The other two died young.'

'Then I could speak to the son? What is his name?' At this point, behind Nargis, Karam saw a hand move the curtain, a woman's face with a finger to her lips appeared then pointed to the door and downwards. Nargis didn't notice: she was moving her legs to a more comfortable seating position and re-arranging the folds of her sari.

'You might have difficulty speaking with him. He is dumb.' Her voice had become cold now.

'Then I have been misinformed. I've wasted your time.'

'Not at all. Will I see you again? Do come again this evening. I will be singing.'

'That would indeed be a pleasure. I will certainly come, if business allows.'

'Too much work is not good for a man. Come and see me - any time.'

'I would be honoured.' Karam rose, trying to hide the stiffness in his legs. She makes me want to be young again, he thought.

She rang the bell at her side. A girl of about ten came into the room. 'See the gentleman out, Kavita.' Nargis rose slowly to open her curtains and the breeze blew in.

The girl accompanied him down the first flight of stairs but at the open door of the second room was draped a voluptuous figure in white satin, long silky hair over her shoulders, fair skin, high cheek-bones, full red lips, she stretched out one beautiful long leg to bar his way. With one hand she waved off the girl and with the other beckoned him into the dimly candle-lit room.

Nargis appeared at the top landing, 'Jasmine, you never miss a trick. You've got half-an-hour then it's dance practice.'

Jasmine flicked her scarf up to her madam, leading Karam into her room.

He stood behind the closed door and thought, Jasmine, the dancer from last evening. Quick to take advantage.

He watched her move around the room, graceful in her long kaftan, lighting more candles, checking the curtains were closed. Then she picked up a tall candlestick, brought it to the drawer of her almirah and pulling it open, put her finger to her lips and stared into Karam's eyes. Her finger pointed down into the drawer as Karam moved towards it. There was a photograph and from it, gazing up at him ... his sister? He looked up at Jasmine, beginning to speak but as her fingers instantly covered his lips, she mouthed a 'no' at him. He leaned on the almirah and looked down again; this time he lifted the photograph. It was of postcard size showing a young woman sitting at a desk with her right arm on the desk and her left at her side, a rose in her hand. Jasmine leaned over and whispered in his ear 'Nur'.

Of course, it had to be, thought Karam, but why the denial from Nargis?

Jasmine crooked her finger at him, moving towards her bed she lifted a large sand timer that sat on her bedside table and turned it over to measure his time with her. She came over to him, taking his hand and pulling him over to the table on the other side of the bed and offered him - ah, he knew the drug – more potent than wine. He took two pods and chewed quickly.

She whispered in his ear, 'Do not speak. Listen. I know where Nur is. Trust me. But if we do no business here the madam will suspect.' She moved to his other ear, 'Put the money on the table. Ten. It's not too much, really - I'm good.' She pulled away and grinned at him, at the same time unhooking the front of her kaftan and slipping it away from her shoulders to the floor.

Karam removed his jacket and placed it round the back of a chair. Taking out his wallet he counted the required amount and left it on the table. When he turned, she was lying stretched out naked on the bed, on her side with her head in her left hand, her hair falling between her breasts, with that same mischievous grin on her lips. The drug was taking a hold on him now, he felt twenty-five again. Was he that age the last time he was in this room? Was he fifteen when he was here the first time or later when he brought Basant? So young, we were all so young ...

CHAPTER FOUR

Rurka 1906

His brother died as the cock crowed to greet the morning and the cold winter sun rose to wake the sleeping village. Those waiting around the unconscious man had lowered him to the floor as tradition decreed. They now gave instructions to his fifteen-year old brother.

'Go now, Basant. Fetch your neighbour and cousins.'

'Have the funeral pyre prepared.'

'And bring the reader of the Holy Book with you.'

Adjusting his over-blanket around his turbaned head and sweeping it across his left shoulder, Basant crossed the narrow courtyard to the door in four long strides. Once over the threshold his body shook with sobs. He leaned against the window, bending like a sapling in a high wind, taking deep breaths and trying not to moan. It seemed longer but in a minute he'd pulled himself up. Squaring his shoulders and stretching to his full height he walked, with a steady gait, away from the house to the other side of the well around which the houses were built; all similar consisting of a courtyard with one large room behind and a store behind that. As the land was needed for crops, space for living was limited. All the walls adjoined each other and the flat roofs created extra space above the cramped lanes. The smell of burning buffalo-dung and wood was in the air; the potters' donkeys brayed for food, buffalo and cows lowed for the person who milked them, but Basant hardly heard these familiar morning sounds. On reaching his neighbour's house he stopped, sighed and pushed at the door, rattling the chain that kept it closed on the inside.

As soon as it opened, he blurted out, 'It's my brother … the plague has taken him.'

The middle-aged man standing in the small yard only nodded in answer, at the same time turning to call for his son. Together the three of them walked back towards Basant's house, then he turned into the lane on his right leading to the centre of the village, and they entered the dwelling of the deceased man.

Until the sun was overhead it would be cold so the men he met were wrapped in light blankets over their rough cotton pyjama trousers and shirts, their heads were covered with turbans or felt hats. He felt self-conscious though only his eyes were visible; they marked him out as different. Pale grey tinged with pink eyes, pale skin, white eyelashes; people might forget his name but not that he was an albino.

He stopped at two more houses, those of his second cousins, to convey the sad news, before making his way through the lanes to the untouchable quarter where Ram lived. Their families had been connected for generations; the lower caste cleaners had always prepared the funeral pyres for Basant's family, who were carpenters. Ram's wife would clean the house and dispose of the dead man's clothes and bedding. Since he had died of the plague all his personal effects would be burned. Ram was as old as Basant's father and stood now, with the youth, outside the one room that was his home.

'My sympathies are with you. Now you must take your brother's place as the provider, for the sake of your sister. And there is a child?'

41

'Yes, I am now responsible for my sister Bhani and my niece Easrie,' answered Basant.

'Times are hard but with God's help you will win through,' replied Ram. 'You were always a good worker, even as a child.'

Basant lifted his gaze from the wall, 'Well, I'll see you at the cremation grounds.'

He heard a woman's voice from inside the room, 'After I've cleared up, I'll come to your house, Basant.' She was hidden from his view, although he could see two boys, sitting on floor-mats beside her cooking fire.

He returned to his house via the Sikh temple with the reader of the Holy Book, and as they entered, the men and women in the courtyard turned to look towards them. A prayer consisting of God's names, 'Satnam Waheguru', was being chanted and whilst quietly murmuring the men now carried the body for ritual washing at the 'wet' corner of the house, near the door leading into the lane. Thick canes of bamboo were fashioned into a bier on which the shroud-covered body was placed. The reader greeted the elders of Basant's extended family with words of condolence. The cousins Basant had called on were now entering the crowded courtyard, so that some people moved into Basant's uncles' house, through a connecting door.

The women nearest the body were wives of uncles and cousins of the dead man as all his girl-cousins were married and lived in other villages. His ten-year old sister sat in the back room where his young wife lay in a fever. The older women wept in high keening voices that sounded like wind in a storm, their rhythmic slapping of chests and thighs the waves crashing on rocks. There were surges of weeping as each new member of the group arrived and they called out to the dead man's spirit.

42

'Where have you gone?'

'You're leaving a young baby and a wife.'

Wailing, slapping ...

'She also has the plague.'

'Your baby will be orphaned.'

In between the weeping, the hushed worries ...

'There were ten deaths in the village yesterday. The cremation grounds are very busy.'

'Will the plague never end?'

'It is a pity my sister-in-law can't see him for the last time,' said Bhani as her niece clung to her, afraid of the noise.

Someone answered, 'No, poor girl, she is so ill.'

'It is time,' the eldest of Basant's aunts looked towards the men, 'Take him away now.'

The reader began to recite the evening prayer for the dead man. Basant and the others stood barefoot and with covered heads for with the prayers, they believed the Guru was there in spirit. At the end, everyone kneeled and touched their foreheads to the ground. The women sat down, as six men lifted the bier onto their shoulders. The reader took his place at the front of the small procession, chanting God's name in a clear voice. As they moved away Bhani placed the baby on the ground, slapped her hands to her forehead, in imitation of the older women, and rose towards her brother's body. A woman stepped in front of her and others pulled her down to sit; only men performed the last rites of the dead. With slow steps the small procession walked into the lane. The houses on both sides were quiet, with doors closed, because the word was out that there had been a death and everyone knew not to cross the path of a funeral. The villagers feared that taking too much interest would encourage their own misfortune; in the wider bazaar people quickly stepped into the shadows, closing doors and venturing out only after sounds of the chanting had passed.

At the cremation site there were a few burnt out pyres but one new space where Ram was waiting. The wood for the pyre had been taken from the communal pile which the lower caste villagers, the cleaners and tanners, gathered every day. Five six-foot long logs were already in place on the ground and, as the group approached five smaller logs were laid across the first. The body was positioned over these, with medium length logs placed on top, in a criss-cross pattern.

'It will be a good burning,' Ram declared. 'There is the right amount of wood and it's dry.'

An unfired clay pot was broken on the head of the body. Basant did not know why this was done, but he suspected it was a precaution against burning anyone alive. He was given a lighted stick and walked round the pyre starting the blaze. His heart felt heavy; his head buzzed with memories of past funerals. Both his parents had been cremated here. The words from the Holy Book were repeated by the reader: 'All are sent by God. When He calls we return.' Wherever God was, perhaps the souls of his parents and brother were there now. He was oblivious of the others around the burning pyre and of the tears that streamed down his face.

He remembered the building of their house. His father had fitted the window casements with wooden shutters; his uncles built the adjoining house in the space at the back. Everyone had been happy. He remembered his brother teaching him how to spin a top in the lane whilst his mother had laughed, standing in the doorway with a broom in her hand. He had felt safe, as if nothing would change. How wrong could he have been?

His gaze was still fixed on the ground when he became aware of someone speaking. Realising he'd lost track of time and the pyre in front of him had burnt low, he looked up with a start, shielding his eyes from the morning sun.

'Let us return to the temple,' directed the reader.

'I will wait here until the ashes are cold. Will you be here in the morning to gather the remains?' Ram looked over at Basant, who nodded.

The reader placed his hand on the boy's shoulder, leading him away.

By the time the men had returned to Basant's house, it was mid-morning. The house had been ritually cleaned and the dead man's few clothes, his sheets and quilt, had been removed by the untouchable woman. Neighbours had cooked food and brought it to the house, but the bereaved family could not eat as the young woman whose husband's body had been cremated that morning lay, hardly conscious, in the back room. Her baby played in the courtyard as Basant came in and sat down cross-legged on a mat near her.

'Look, she can stand now,' said Bhani.

He held out his arms and nodded to the child, 'Come to me. Come here, Easrie.'

She left her aunt's arms, making gurgling sounds, took a tottering step towards him, and fell. He lifted her up and smiled with tight lips for the sadness was still heavy on him. She deserved a better start in life and now that he was the head of his family he would do everything he could to make her happy.

Bhani looked at him seeming to read his thoughts. It was not difficult for her to accept him as the head of the family. He was five years her elder and had always been serious about his duties.

45

'Her mother is failing. Does her family know she is so ill?'

'Uncle has sent a message to Mehatpur Village about our brother's death. Her father should be here in an hour or two.'

And he was. Dara Singh sat with his unconscious daughter through the night, until she took her last breath. He held her baby and knew what he must do for the little one. Her aunt Takri would come here, to help look after her. True there was Bhani two years younger than Takri, a child-widow at present but she could be placed in marriage in the future, leaving the baby alone so, it was best that Takri should marry Basant as tradition decreed.

Early the next morning Basant went to the cremation ground to gather his brother's ashes, and then retraced the previous day's steps with almost the same group of men, but this time they carried a young woman's body. His baby niece, Easrie, had now lost both her parents. On their return from the funeral the men sat on low stools in the courtyard, the women in the room behind. Tea was brewing on the fire in the lean-to, under the wooden ladder.

'I tell you what, I'd like some of that tea,' said Dara, 'it smells good.'

'I'll pour some for you.' Basant rose and gave a brass tumbler of tea to each of his uncles as well as to Dara. Brewed with cardamom and cloves it tasted spicy, warm and soothing. Dara was a man who would come straight to the point when required and he felt, in his present situation, there was no time to waste. He looked at the uncles.

'My daughter and son-in-law have gone from this world,' he began. 'My grand-daughter is left without parents. It is a time of sadness but God's plan must be accepted. I would like to talk about the future?'

The two men nodded, as they knew how families bonded following deaths.

'As you know, I was widowed and my wife passed away leaving me our four daughters. I thought I was fortunate that two of the girls were now married and happy but now one of them is no more. However to keep the link between our families intact, I am willing to marry my third daughter to Basant. She is young, twelve years old, but she is able to do all the housework, and will take responsibility for the baby. What is your opinion?'

He addressed this to Basant's elder uncle who looked at his brother for support. A hardly discernible nod encouraged him to continue.

'We have no objection. An empty place must be filled, a child needs a mother. Who would be more fitting than your daughter for my nephew's wife? What about you Basant? Have you anything to say?'

The young man knew the expected reply. His upbringing was steeped in duty and responsibility to the family. This was how he had lived throughout his young life and he accepted that there was no other way. At least he had seen Takri, and she was lovely, so she might have more difficulty accepting him; she would be called the wife of the albino. However, if this was what their families wished then there was pressure on both of them to agree. She might grow to like him, and if she didn't, then he would still have to live with her.

'I will do as my elders wish,' he said quietly lowering his eyes towards the mud-smoothed floor.

'It is settled,' his uncle raised his voice. 'You must return home, Dara, and make preparations. With the help of the Brahmin choose an auspicious date and we will bring the bridegroom to your village. Your daughter will be welcome in our family.'

At this point, having heard the discussion, the aunts with faces veiled, and Bhani who as a daughter of the house, did not cover her face from the men, joined the group and Dara brought from his pocket the handkerchief in which his money was wrapped. Taking a coin he rose and waved it in a clockwise direction over Basant's head, before putting it into the youth's lap where his aunt had hurriedly placed a scarf. He completed the little ritual by placing both hands on his future son-in-law's head in blessing. Turning to the family he bowed, and took his leave.

CHAPTER FIVE

Mehatpur 1906

The five miles to Mehatpur, Dara's village, were not a long walk but, about a mile down the road, an ox-cart overtook him.

'Ohay! Stop here! Halt, I say!' The driver was a land worker, son of a Jat friend.

'Karam! How are you, my boy?' shouted Dara.

'Ah, I'm well, Dara Uncle. I was hoping for company on the road back home.' Karam grinned, with his free arm emptying the space beside him of its sacks. The cart was a large two-wheeled, flat board pulled by a pair of slim white single-humped oxen.

'I've just delivered some grain, and I'm taking these seed potatoes to Father.'

'So I see. How is your father?'

'He is well. Ohay! Hutt, hutt, keep straight you two!' The oxen shook their heads from side to side, setting the bells round their necks ringing. The fields along the road were brown with neat rows of green shoots about a foot high stretching up under the warm, afternoon sun.

'What are these rumours I've heard about you?' Dara asked once he was settled.

'Yes, I'm going to Calcutta. That's where the money is now, Uncle. The land can't support all of us: you've found work in Karachi. I have an older brother who will look after the crops, so why would I stay?'

'You're quite right about life here. The only choices are the land, the army or the city.'

'Who knows, from Calcutta I might get away to Singapore. Then I'll return a very rich man,' Karam laughed.

'Yes, indeed. Going east seems to be the way, nowadays. Good luck to you, son. I've also heard you're keen on politics. Be careful.'

A boy goatherd called to his charges, a long line of brown and white nanny goats and kids, to keep to the side, at the same time waving to Karam to overtake them. The jingling of bells mingled with the sound of bleating and the soft rhythm of oxen hooves on the ground.

'Are you attending the memorial for the First War of Independence, Uncle? It's being organised by the Congress party in the village.'

'Like your father, Karam, I'm too cautious. So they're calling the mutiny the 'First War of Independence' now?'

'It was the British who called it the Mutiny. It was the first combined insurgence against them. If only ...'

'Sikhs hadn't joined forces with the British?' Dara finished.

'And become their 'pet' warriors. That's what's happened.'

'Yes, aren't you proud that your father was a subedar, a captain in the Indian Army?'

'Yes, but he couldn't be equal to the British officers. There are two promotion structures just as there is within the government and the law. It's demoralising for me, and other

50

young people, knowing Indians like us can only reach a certain level while the British are here.'

Yes, I understand, but this fight is not for me. I only want to live my life in peace. We work with the land; your caste manages the crops, mine provides the appropriate tools and our lives are governed by the seasons, so does it matter who the rulers are - the educated Indians or the British?' Dara gazed around at the fields, some green with the early sugar cane, some newly furrowed and brown; the land he loved.

'India is our country, we'll win it back. I've joined the Congress party, Uncle,' announced Karam.

'Alright, ha ha haa,' laughed Dara bowing his head to the optimism of youth. 'Good luck to you, son. You are at the spring of your life and I ... well, I am at the autumn and I have responsibilities,' he smiled. Putting his arm around the younger man's shoulders he gave a strong squeeze.

Karam bent his head, at the same time pointing his hand down to Dara's feet. 'Give me your blessing, Uncle.'

'May you live long, and be prosperous.' Dara gave the designated blessing and alighting from the cart, strode towards his house. He stopped at the village meeting place for men at the crossroads, under the massive shade of the ancient banyan tree. He washed his hands, taking a drink at the community water pump before sitting on a mat beside the village elders who discussed and sympathised with his loss. Then conversation turned to news, mainly of the plague, the price of grain and the audacious behaviour of the young.

It was late when he arrived home, as his daughter Takri lit the cooking fire of wood and cow dung patties, while there was still an afternoon sun, and before the temperature dropped. He closed the door in the courtyard behind him and turned towards the lean-to which covered the cooking area, behind it was the main room with a store at the very back. A small earthenware oil lamp was lit in the room and he guessed that his youngest daughter was asleep otherwise she would have run to him. Above on the flat roofs of the village could be heard the sound of children shouting over their flying kites and mothers calling them to come downstairs to bed.

He nodded to his mother and gazed sadly at Takri.

'It was a shock when Basant's cousin came with the news this morning. It seems like yesterday she played in this house.' Takri's grandmother whose low stool was near the fire, where she could supervise her grand-daughter, wiped away tears. She had thought she'd cried enough that day, but the sight of her son, widowed and now a daughter also dead, renewed them.

'Yes. The plague has Rurka in its grip,' Dara answered as he took the blanket from his shoulder, hanging it on a peg near the door of the room.

'It is God's will, my son,' the old woman was resigned.

'The houses are small, the lanes narrow and people do not keep the open gutters clean,' continued Dara, letting his anger hide the pain of his daughter's death. He went to the wet corner near the door to wash.

'It is our kismet,' she felt the frustration in his voice, and spoke to appease it.

Takri sat on her low wooden stool and hugged her knees, staring into the flames half-listening to their conversation.

'Sometimes kismet needs a helping hand; we make our own luck, I believe. Is there any food, Mother?' He rubbed his arms with soap.

'There are chapattis, cooked potatoes and some dhal. Our neighbours are kind.'

'We will do the same for them when the time comes. As it will, there is no doubt of that,' Dara returned to the fire area.

Takri thought of her sister, for whom she had cried all day, but now her tears had dried up. When her father asked for food, she straightened her back, adjusted her dupatta around her shoulders and stoked the fire. On the three low walls surrounding it she placed the earthenware pot containing the neighbours' offerings. Her father sat down on a hessian mat near her. He ate silently, afterwards drinking the water from the brass tumbler that Takri placed next to the tray. Indicating satisfaction with a loud belch, he washed his fingers with the remaining water, letting it fall into his empty bowl.

Turning to his mother he said, 'It may have been somewhat forward of me, so close to the funerals, but I told them of my decision about the future of Takri and the baby.'

'Of course, you are a concerned father. Our neighbours were saying the same thing today.'

Someone cleared his throat at the door, more an announcement than a personal necessity; a rattling of the chain and Dara's friend and neighbour came in.

'I'm so sorry to hear about your daughter,' he approached the three sitting round the fire, 'Seems only yesterday she was married. I would have come with you but there was so much work in the fields.'

Dara reached to the wall to a propped up low stool, placing it beside him, motioning to his neighbour to be seated, at the same time replying sadly, 'No-one wants their child to die. The plague is a curse, you know, though when death comes we are powerless.'

After a pause, he added, 'Are the potatoes being planted?'

'Yes, but I have two broken cartwheels to repair.'

Dara nodded, 'I'll help you, tomorrow. Tell me, has your son written from Delhi? How is he? I was reminded of him when I met Karam this morning. You know, the retired subedar's son? He's planning on leaving too.'

Takri raised her head at the mention of Karam. She wondered that she should be so interested in a boy from her village and admonished herself.

'Karam is a farmer what will he do in the city? My son is well, and there is much work for the skilled castes. The British are planning many buildings and roads for the new capital - New Delhi, it's to be called. Certainly it's the place to be for a young working man.'

Turning to Dara's mother, he asked, 'Mother, how is your health?'

'I am as well as the times, and my age, permits. The younger girl has a temperature today, but I'm sure she'll be up and about again, tomorrow. No swelling under her arms, so she is clear of the plague. Thank God.'

Takri had brewed some spiced tea, while they were talking and offered him some, but he wouldn't have any.

'No, Takri, my child. My wife will have some ready, and she'll wait for me before drinking her own. She thinks it's her marital duty to deprive herself,' he shrugged.

'Perhaps her tea tastes sweeter when you're with her,' the grandmother's eyes twinkled.

'Goodnight, Mother,' he shrugged and smiled, 'See you in the morning, Dara.' With only his eyes visible, wrapped up in his blanket against the advancing evening chill, he left, fastening the latch on the door.

Takri sipped the hot tea and began telling her father of the day's visitors, 'We put sheets down on the floor but there was hardly enough room. Everyone cried and spoke about Sister. Will Grandmother from Nurmahal come early tomorrow, Papa?'

'Yes, I'm sure she will,' replied Dara thinking how distressed his mother-in-law would be at the death of her eldest grandchild.

Takri damped down the fire with a little water, cleaned around the fireplace and went inside to lie down on the bed with her younger sister. She could not sleep as her father's words, 'I have spoken about the future of the little girl and Takri,' kept returning to her mind. The women who had come to sit with her grandmother had also asked, 'What will become of the baby?' She thought of the dead in Rurka and shivered. The plague was killing people there, how could they send her, didn't they care that she might die like her sister? What could she do? She knew everyone thought she should marry Basant who was pitied because of his skin, his eyes and the colour of his hair. She'd always ignored him when he'd visited with his brother. And there was Bhani, the sister, a child-widow who might never re-marry; would that make her bitter and angry, difficult to live with?

They were still talking outside the room but she couldn't make out their words although sometimes her name was mentioned and then, she drifted into a restless sleep, dreaming she was walking towards Rurka surrounded by mist, in tears, hearing footsteps behind her all the way but not seeing anyone and never reaching her destination.

The following morning after breakfast of parathas, lemon pickle and sweet, spiced tea, her grandmother went into the store room. Taking down the smaller, steel trunks she opened the large, wooden dowry chest. It contained all the spare material and bedding she had stored for the next granddaughter's wedding, and now that was Takri. Slowly, she took out the patterned and plain cottons and satins, and matched the shades. Young brides wore the brightest colours. She smiled, but then remembered that being a bride was such a short time in a woman's life. So soon childbirth and illness took its toll, and for many girls there were long years of widowhood, with the wearing of rough white cotton. She wondered whether the practice of suttee, the burning of widows on their husband's funeral pyres, was not a kindness for many widows who endured a slave's life without a husband. The previous year her friend had submitted to suttee, so-called purification; it wasn't completely gone from the community. She hoped her friend had taken drugs before lying down on the pyre. She'd heard there were laws against it but how could peoples' long-held beliefs be changed like that? The two friends had been estranged since their teens; sent to far-off villages in marriage and become busy raising their children. Although she hadn't seen her friend for years it was sad to think of her life ending in that way. Trying to shake off these morbid thoughts she turned to the job in hand -this was a wedding she was preparing for, a happy occasion for her son and a grand-daughter's rite of passage.

She turned her attention to the materials. Fine muslin dupattas, the long scarves that women always draped around their shoulders and head, along with the salwar-kameez that made up the Punjabi suit. She would buy more material for the overskirt, the gaghra, which covered the salwar. Without the overskirt Takri would not be able to walk outside the house in Rurka. She sighed, thinking, she's still a child, hasn't even started her cloths. She must tell Basant's aunts. They'll look after her until she's old enough for all the duties of a bride. As the song says, no sooner are our daughters born it seems, that we send them away to live with strangers.

Takri sat on the bed with her sister, and watched her grandmother. She had something to say, but she knew it was unseemly to be involved in her own wedding preparations. Her grandmother sensed this, and began to explain, all the time pretending to be engrossed in the materials.

'Takri, you will be married very soon. Your sister's brother-in-law Basant is to be your husband. You've seen him?'

The girl frowned at the older woman. Moving closer she drew a deep breath to pluck up courage, and almost inaudibly whispered, 'Ma, there is something wrong with him. He has white hair and there is no colour in his skin, he looks old.'

'Oh. That's the falveri. It's a skin disorder. Basant has no colour in his skin or his hair. The white hair makes him seem old, but his face is young. He is very able in other ways, and there is your sister's child, Takri, to think of. I know it's not a perfect situation, but you love Easrie, and if your sister had lived we would have looked for someone else for you. The decision is made now, it is your kismet. Accept it, child.'

'But Ma, how can you even think of sending me to Rurka when Sister has died in that village?' Takri spoke louder. 'Why can't we just bring Easrie home to live here?'

'Your father has three girls, and to bring Easrie would be another burden on him. As it is, we are fortunate Basant's family do not insist we take her.'

'I would work. You've taught me to sew and knit and weave.'

'Hush, silly girl. You cannot stay here because marriage is your destiny. This is a chance to lighten your father's load.'

'It's not about me then. You don't really care that Sister is dead. It's another load off your shoulders; you want rid of me.' Takri, in tears, rose and left the room to go and sit at the top of the bamboo ladder that led to the roof, where she always felt distanced from everyone, and able to think. Knowing her fate was sealed, and feeling so helpless, all she wanted was to lie in bed with a quilt over her head, but the house was busy with visitors. Everyone thought she was sad because her sister had died, but she was equally upset at the changes being planned for her life. Her younger sister could go to bed early, but she was expected to behave more like an adult.

Later that day, her other grandmother arrived. After a sad reunion the two women talked of Takri's future, and tried to console her. 'It's for the best,' they repeated to her. The next day they called the Brahmin who spent some time poring over old charts, calculating an auspicious date for the wedding. He was given some grain for his contribution. Takri tried to think of the good things about being married. At least she wouldn't wear second-hand clothes: she would have several new outfits from her grandmothers, and more from her in-laws. Then there was Easrie, her niece; she was looking forward to being with her.

The month passed and during the days preceding the wedding, Takri had little to say. As her grandmother had taught her, and as she had seen in the behaviour of her older sisters, it was best to get on with your duties. The task of taking the cotton-filled quilts and sheets up on to the roof to dry in the afternoon sun was finished, and she sat enjoying the heat, on the low wall that separated each house's rooftop. Two girls on a neighbouring roof sat cross-legged on a string bed. One was having her hair checked for nits, then massaged with mustard oil by the other.

Takri thought of girls from rich families who were given dowries of bedding, kitchen-ware and furniture, but she knew her father could not afford these things. Her sisters were only given clothes for themselves and for their new family, and it would be the same for her. There would be a wedding feast for the guests who came with her husband and then they would take her with them to begin a new life.

'You'll be married soon, Takri.' Her cousin's excited whisper shook her out of her thoughts.

'Oh, I didn't hear you approach, Sukhi,' answered Takri.

'I remember Basant from your sister's wedding. He does look very strange, so pink, but you will get used to that. Anyway, in the night it's dark,' she giggled. 'Are his eyes also pink, Takri?'

'How would I know? I haven't looked at him,' retorted Takri with a frown.

'Well, I bet he's looked at you: with your fair skin and light brown eyes, you're a beauty,' Sukhi grinned, pleased with the mischief she was creating.

Takri's cousin was on a return visit from her in-laws, the first visit after the consummation of her marriage. She continued to show off her new knowledge.

'Have you had your cloths, Takri? No? In that case you'll not be allowed to sleep with him.'

Sukhi could ask questions and give the answers as well, Takri thought. She had seen the older women wash cloths every month, and thought she knew why, but she hadn't had to do that yet and anyway no-one talked openly of such things, so she was wasn't sure what it meant.

'I slept with my husband last month, and this is the present he gave me, this locket. Here's his photo in it. Basant must give you something the first time and make sure he does

59

before ... you give him ... yourself. We kept the oil lamp burning. I was so embarrassed, I shut my eyes tight. I don't now though, my husband is so handsome with his fair skin and wavy brown hair.'

Takri wouldn't look up; continuing to twirl her scarf around her fingers. Her cousin became tired of her non-responsiveness, and sauntered over to talk to the girls on the other roof. Glad to be rid of her, Takri climbed down the ladder to resume her chores though Sukhi's words still rankled and set up questions in her mind.

Later in the store room, her sister Tara watched, as Takri began to spread a layer of fine smooth clay over the floor to cover any cracks. The wooden dowry box was lifted off the floor on bricks.

'Tara, don't bother me. Everyone expects me to look sad because I'm leaving, I'm going to do that from now on,' Takri said between long sweeps of her arms over the floor.

'Don't think you're too young, Takri. After all, you're twelve. Bhani was seven when she was married.' Tara ignored the tone of dismissal from the older girl.

'I know that. Bhani was seven when she was married, but she wasn't sent to live with her husband, so she wasn't really a wife when he died. That's why she's called a seventh-year widow. She should be married again.'

'You're wrong! Grandmother says if you think of someone as your husband, then that's what he is. So there! She can't marry again,' exclaimed Tara, stamping her foot.

'Oh, don't be a baby. A man gets married again,' Takri shot an angry look at her younger sister. 'Go away Tara. Up on the roof, Grandmother is there.'

Tara pouted and left, making as much noise as she could by throwing the wooden fan in her hand into the corner. Later that evening, Takri heard her father and grandmother at the fireplace talking about the plans for her wedding. In a small house it was difficult to avoid other conversations. She sat on the bed, sewing a pillowcase.

'Will we have enough provisions for the wedding feast?' her grandmother asked.

'Yes, the neighbours are a great help. And the overnight bedding for the wedding party is ready at the gurdwara. We will bring the Holy Book from there and have the wedding ceremony on the roof. One overnight stay is enough, as we are still mourning,' Dara replied.

And so it begins, thought Takri with a sigh.

Cooking of the sweets, and preparation for the meals, began a week before the wedding day with each caste taking up their own duties whether these were preparation, cleaning or distribution. The first sweets were placed in one end of Takri's dupatta, to be distributed by her to guests and neighbours.

Takri's mother's family arrived. Her grandmother, one uncle, three aunts and four children got together, with the neighbourhood women, to give Takri's skin a rubbing of turmeric and mustard oil paste. This cleansing was the first ceremony of several. She sat quietly in the courtyard, on a piece of wood in front of the rangoli pattern on the ground, amidst the hustle and bustle. The women around her were talking to everyone at the same time. Takri thought that they liked the sound of their own voices. Nothing was expected of her so she could sit quietly, and look on.

'Eh hai hai, this rangoli pattern is so plain. It needs more colour.'

'I haven't finished. I've got some more coloured flour here,' was the reply.

'Come on everyone. Bring the red cover and hold it here, above Takri's head.'

'Maji, is that enough paste?'

'It looks very dry. It needs more oil.'

'No, it's fine.'

'It is almost quarter to the hour, the auspicious time, so we must start now.'

'Have you called everyone, Marassen?' This was the caste title of the Muslim woman.

Takri looked at her and wondered if everyone of that caste was a talented musician, since that was their work. It was also her duty to go round all the homes of the extended family and give oral invitations for every meal they ate at the wedding house.

'You are invited to Takri's mendhi ceremony this morning,' she had said.

At lunch it would be, 'You have an invitation to lunch.'

Everyone knew who was invited, but to be called to eat by the Marassen was the personal touch.

'Oh yes. I did that this morning,' she smiled, 'and everyone is here.'

Takri listened, as the Marassen led the singing. She thought of her mother who would have been the first to be sung the 'many happy returns' wishes of this occasion. But everyone was careful not to mention her, or Takri's dead sister.

The singing continued, with the names of all who were there, as the women took turns to rub the paste into Takri's arms, legs, face and feet which she thought was fun and ticklish. Everyone was congratulated except Takri; she felt alone and thought of her mother. She was told to rise, and her grandmother completed the final rite of the ceremony by smearing the remaining paste on the palms of her own hands and walking out of the front door to make hand prints on the wall outside, either side of the front door.

The women followed her out to watch, smiling and nodding in the spring sunshine. The prints marked the house as an abode of celebration. Green leaves of the neem tree were hung on a string above the threshold to bring good luck to everyone who passed under them. Dara and his brother and cousins arrived to a chorus of congratulations from the women and the servant castes demanded money from him since he was so fortunate as to be having a wedding for his daughter. He emptied his pockets of the coins they contained and handed them out.

That evening the women returned to the house to sing traditional wedding songs. The musician brought the drum and the singing lasted until midnight in the glow of oil lamps. Coins were waved around Takri's head and given to the drummer. At last the women returned to their own homes, smiling and happy, with handfuls of fried flour and sugar sweets.

Takri could not sleep. It was partly the excitement, but added to that, she was not accustomed to sitting still for so long. As the bride she couldn't work or go outside the house after the cleansing ceremony. She had escaped, in the late afternoon, wearing her red bangles and red and gold dupatta, upstairs to the roof. It was then she saw someone she knew, someone who could bring a smile to her face just with a look. She watched him as he walked across the rooftops of four houses on the pretext of inspecting the tops of the parapet.

At the sight of him, Takri's thoughts flew back to the previous year at the sugar cane harvest when they had chewed so much of the sweet crop, and become uncontrollably merry. They'd played games all day long: the adults too busy to notice. She wanted to run to those fields and stay near him forever. It was as if she was two people, one screaming to be let free and the other insisting on being sensible. The scream died in her heart; she struggled to breathe evenly. Don't cry; no tears, no tears: eyes on the ground, he'd reached her side and was speaking.

'I'm sorry you have to be married so soon. I thought you'd be around a bit longer,' he spoke with his own eyes to the ground. That voice.

'It is my kismet.' Takri hated the word but had heard her grandmother say it so often, it seemed safe.

'If we meet again, you won't ignore me, will you? We used to play together; in these lanes and the fields. I won't forget you.'

'Of course, I'll remember you.' Takri glanced at his face and saw such sadness. One last look with his green-brown eyes, then he turned, head down, shoulders hunched, stumbling over the rooftop. She watched his feet then looked up at the beaten form of him. With all her might she remained rooted to the spot. As he walked down the wooden steps a voice called, 'Karam, come and eat, son. You're late.'

Legs trembling, feeling a soft pain in her chest, Takri sank onto the rooftop, dropping her head to her knees. Tears soaked into her salwar. It was not fair that life changed this much just because she was a girl. Perhaps if Karam hadn't looked like that she might have managed to ignore her own feelings. Was it possible to go to him, and ask for help: to run away? What a silly idea, they were from different castes from the same village, and would be ridiculed. His family would hate her, and hers would beat him until he died, dragging her back if they didn't kill her as well. The noise from below disturbed her; the lamps had been lit. Wiping her face with her dupatta, she climbed down the ladder, resolved to accept her fate.

The different ceremonies of the wedding became a fleeting memory in which Takri felt like a puppet. When Basant arrived dressed as a bridegroom in a long embroidered coat and red turban, with the wedding party, she was confined to the store room. Most of the women who sat in the room with her were discreet and kind, but she heard whispers about his skin.

'What a pity she is marrying an albino, such a lovely girl.'

'Indeed, she is.'

'They've only agreed because of her sister's baby.'

'It's tragic. We all want a husband who looks like a prince; tall, dark and handsome. Poor girl, she'll not be happy. It's bad kismet.'

The following morning, with her grandmother looking on, her aunts dressed her, singing the traditional wedding verses in which the bride bids farewell to all that's dear to her.

'It is my wedding day; my leaving hour.

Oh milk churn,
In the early mornings, I won't turn
your paddle,
Will you forget me now?

Oh flames, will you still burn when I
no longer

Turn the wood to coax you into
colour?

Oh pigeons flying free above my
rooftop.
Will you still coo with throbbing
throats?
Look for me and wonder why
I'm not there to bring your daily grain?

*No sooner am I born than they come to
take me away;*
*Those cruel ones, how will I grow to love
them?*

And now, too soon, I am inside,
dressed in blood-red satin.
The henna, dark maroon and beautiful,
on my hands and feet
See how the red-gold threads in my
hair glisten in the lamp light.
The mirror in my hand shows
a transformation, I glance and look away
I am the girl who plays in the corn, not that
woman.

Those mistresses of compromise;
keepers of the rites of passage,
The women sing to me,

'May you always be a wife

may colour pervade your life
until the very day you die.

Let us adorn you with these earrings;
these globes, feminine and fair,
dropping to your neck. See, your
mother's heart trembles
as she kisses her innocent girl.

We roll the bangles on your arms,
attach coconuts, earth symbols.
May all you desire be yours, as we send
you forward to your new life

Here is the ornament for your
forehead; the bridal jewel, it sparkles!
We are the bride-givers; our duty is to
give.

Place your feet on this cushion; let us
tie the bells on your fine ankles, your
hennaed feet, so pretty with rose-
tipped nails.

Almost ready. Stand up, let us place
your embroidered covering over you,
veil your face, beautiful as the silver
moon.

'May you always be a wife,
may colour pervade your life

until the very day you die.

Takri tried not to listen to the words, not to think of leaving. As the words of the song had indicated the band played to announce the arrival of the wedding party, she was ready and her uncle helped her to ascend the ladder, and carried her over to the raised dais on which was placed the Holy Book. He set her down, on the mat in front of it, next to Basant. He sat looking at the Holy Book. The musicians played and the reader turned to the pages of the wedding service; the hymns which guided the couple in the religious life of the future.

Then Takri, enveloped in her blanket, heard her name mentioned, 'Takri, daughter of Dara Singh who is to marry ...' she thought that's right, it's me, this is happening to me.

Someone put the end of a scarf into her hand, she knew it was her father; the scarf would be around Basant's shoulder, with the other end in his hand. She had not seen him; the elders who were the witnesses, could be trusted to make certain that all was, as it should be. The couple listened, made obeisance after each stanza, and were deemed to be married when the fourth was read. The musicians, accompanied by a tabla drum and harmonium, sang the hymn, 'Oh, Father, I am married.' She was given the communal sweet and helped downstairs.

There was such a commotion in the rooms. The women were congratulating Takri's grandmother. Her younger sister and cousins now came closer to her since the ceremony was over and everyone was able to relax.

The men went to the gurdwara for the wedding feast. Takri remained in the back room where a tray of food was brought to her. Then, after another interminable wait, during which she grew quite anxious as she knew the next step was the leaving. Basant came into the room and they were given a sweet to eat, she was handed the end of his scarf to hold again helped to stand and walk behind him for a few steps. She could only see her own two feet in the circle of light that her heavy veil let through.

Then her grandmother gave her rice and said, 'Throw it behind you, Takri. God bless you, dear.' The women sang,

No sooner am I born than they come to take me away;
Those cruel ones, how will I grow to love them?

Hark! The band strikes up,
witnesses assemble,
the bridegroom dressed in red and gold
approaches to lead his bride away.

I throw the rice behind me to the corners of the room, may those who live here never go hungry. I wish you wealth and happiness. I take nothing.

Father, Hark! The very walls of your dwelling tremble at my leaving.
Oh Father, bound by convention.
See! Your darling sits in the palanquin weeping.
A pariah now: a stranger who was once your darling.

She felt herself being hugged by the women, carried weeping and veiled, to the palanquin. There was some rough jolting as it was lifted and then pushed by her father and uncles, the traditional 'sending off'. Takri heard the brass band playing and the palanquin moved away from her childhood home. There were voices but she only made out, 'Basant, come to the front.'

At the end of the lane, Takri knew it would be bright and colourful with paper bunting, ox drawn carts waited to take the wedding party back to Rurka. The oxen were covered in embroidered cloths for the occasion. Bells around their necks rang, adding to the festive atmosphere. The palanquin, with Takri in it, was placed on a cart. The barber's wife and one of Takri's male cousins, who took the place of the brother she did not have, sat on the cart alongside her. The woman opened the palanquin's red and gold curtains, attempting to console Takri who stopped crying, lifting her veil to look at the passing fields.

On reaching Rurka, at the Mansapuri lane, the men took the palanquin from the cart with Basant walking alongside. Trumpets and flutes played to announce their arrival. The neighbours were out on their thresholds or on the rooftops for a good view, and here too there was colourful bunting, the street was scrubbed clean, to welcome the return of the wedding party with the new bride. Basant's aunts, sister and cousins waited at the door of his house. Takri was helped to alight from the palanquin and the welcome ceremony of passing a jug of milk and water around the couple's heads was performed. Basant smiled at everyone, but Takri could only see the circle of ground in front of her feet. Bride and groom were taken inside the house, and after briefly sitting together on the floor, they were separated. The barber-caste chaperone stayed close to Takri at all times, until the next day when a return trip to Mehatpur was arranged. After that Takri and Basant were looked upon as a married couple, but the time for the consummation of their marriage was a decision the elders would make at a much later date.

CHAPTER SIX

Delhi 1906-1908

According to the caste he was born into, Basant was a carpenter and an iron-worker: in Rurka he was an apprentice who made and repaired farm tools. His light skin and white hair usually caused people to look twice at him, but when they became used to the strangeness, it was not a problem. He was good with his hands, interested in people and valued by his fellow workers. One morning he stopped work to listen to an ex-colleague on leave from his job in Delhi.

He asked, 'Could I find work there? Will you take me with you when you return to the city?'

'You'll find work as they're building a whole new city. I have no objection to your coming along, but what about your family?' asked Tirath Singh, a small wiry man, who always wore a black turban.

'My uncles live in the adjoining house to mine in Mansapuri Lane. I will ask them.'

'Yes, I know your uncles. One of them is away in Lahore.'

'That's right. They will look after my family. There's my wife, my sister and my niece. From Delhi, I can bring home more money, and there will be less to worry about.'

In the evening, as was his habit, Basant went through the door in his courtyard to his uncles' house to talk about the day.

He told his elder uncle his plan, how this was an opportunity for him to gain experience, to earn more money.

'It won't be easy, Basant. You're still a learner in your trade.'

'I'll work hard and pay attention to the master carpenters. New Delhi is being built; there will never be another time like this.'

'Yes, I know you will work diligently. If you really want to go, then we are here to support Bhani and Takri. Now, if you become homesick you shouldn't think you must stay there to save face.'

'I'll come back if I need to, but I won't disappoint you either, Uncle.'

It was customary to speak through a chaperone until physical marital relations were allowed, so Basant spoke to Bhani, knowing Takri would be listening. The brother and sister were sitting on the bed in the front room, with baby Easrie sleeping between them while Takri sat on a low stool finishing the stitching of a new little frock. While speaking he glanced over towards Takri hoping she would like his plan. Over the three months since their wedding he had begun to believe his luck had changed; the girl who was his wife was so beautiful and kind. If he wanted to say anything to her he would say, 'Bhani, tell your Bhabi,' for that was the title for brother's wife and how he'd heard his older uncle speak to his wife using his younger uncle. As soon as he would say this, Takri would glance at him and that look made his heart skip a beat. If only he could put his arms around her as he wished but Bhani and Easrie were always there. It was an unspoken rule that there was no touching in company.

This is another good reason to go away; to help us grow up, he thought.

He said, 'I've decided to go to Delhi to work. In a few days, I'll be leaving. Don't look so surprised, we'll have lots of money when I come back.'

'We'll miss you,' said Bhani.

'I'll build another room upstairs and a proper staircase instead of a ladder, with the money I'll earn. It's a great opportunity,' Basant was hopeful and enthusiastic as he glanced at Takri whose eyes met his.

'A proper stair, instead of the ladder?' his sister smiled.

'Yes, then we'll have a wedding for you: I'll be able to give you lots of presents. Everything you want.'

'No. I'm not going to marry again,' Bhani looked away.

'Alright, I didn't mean to upset you. Anyway we'll be better off. I'll be back before either of you know it.'

The next day Bhani asked Takri, 'Do you feel sad that Basant is going?'

'No, I hardly see him. We have not spoken to each other, so why would I be sad? Everyone must find work.'

Secretly, she felt there would be a gap when he was not there every day, but she knew that many women endured these separations. She laid out shirts, pyjama trousers, turbans as well as undergarments for him to pack. On the morning of his departure, Bhani brought in pails of water from the well outside of the house, while Basant tied his clothes into a bundle, and his bedding into a roll. He stood the rope bed on its side at the wet corner and using it as a barrier wall, soaped himself, splashed water all over and put on clean clothes. After combing his long hair, he tied it into a knot on the top of his head, with a tiny

74

semi-circular wooden comb to keep it in place, covering it with his turban, a five metre length of muslin cloth. Taking up his bundle, he bent to touch the feet of his aunts and uncle who were there to see him off, put his arm around Bhani's shoulders to hug her, patted Easrie's head, nodded at Takri, hoped his uncle would approve and picking up his bedding, left the courtyard.

Tirath met him on the main road from where they managed to hitch a lift with a cart driver to the station in Goraya. There was quite a crowd waiting for the Delhi Express. Basant felt apprehensive, he'd never been away from Rurka before, but he told himself men were always leaving. It was because his brother was dead and that made him the head of the family, so he could decide to go and this was a good way to leave the confines of the village behind. It was certainly exciting. He sat on his roll of bedding, and looked around him. Leaving his own bundles near Basant, Tirath walked down the platform to his left wondering if there was anyone he knew amongst the waiting passengers.

From Basant's right a group of noisy young men entered the station. As he was short-sighted he didn't recognise them until they came nearer to him: they were from Takri's village.

'Ah, it is our brother-in-law,' they shouted, slapping his shoulder and shaking hands with him in turn. He smiled at them thinking it was true that when you married you became related to the whole village. Basant especially remembered Karam, a neighbour of Takri's, who had helped serve food at their wedding. He was a cheerful, confident young man; tall, broad-shouldered with laughing green-brown eyes. Basant smiled up at him, somewhat enviously, trying to shut down the thought that he was inferior because of his colour, his height and what else?

75

His shoulders sagged slightly but he pulled up as the other youths continued talking and pacing on the platform.

'I'm actually heading for Calcutta, but I'll stop in Delhi for a while,' Karam told Basant after he'd introduced his two friends who were cousins. He wanted to ask after Takri, but knew this might be inappropriate. It was a strange wedding: everyone knew it was a mismatch, a few whispers about her tall graceful beauty, even at twelve years of age, and with a husband who was small, white-haired with poor sight. What was her life like now with this ... freak? No, he hadn't meant to think that, if he hadn't liked Basant he would have avoided him at the station. Takri's father had agreed to the marriage and Basant seemed kind and generous – what else did a woman want? But he'd dreamed once that he'd brought a bride to his mother's door amidst sounds of music and laughter. But when he'd raised the bride's red and gold veil, the eyes looking up at him were Takri's and he'd woken in a sweat.

He would be careful to keep these thoughts to himself, and that was easy because the men around him never talked of love except to tease each other. Feeling that he should say something he settled for, 'How is everyone at home?' To which Basant replied, 'Fine.' And the moment passed.

The newcomers bent to touch Tirath's feet when he joined them, and he gave the requisite blessing, 'live long'. He was pleased to have their company on the trip; there was safety in numbers, and young men could be an asset, if they didn't cause any trouble in their exuberance.

The train pulled up in a flurry of smoke and screeching brakes. They had two minutes to board: all rushed to find places to sit. The carriage was packed with travellers, mostly men and boys, as the women and girls, those who could afford it, were in a carriage to themselves. Tirath sat down, letting the young men find suitable spaces for their baggage around him: they preferred to stand.

'Near the entrance is best,' declared Karam. 'It's too hot in here.'

'Don't climb on top, it's dangerous,' shouted Tirath, but they didn't hear, only Basant who was at the end of the line turned to give him a shrug accompanied by a sheepish grin.

The journey passed without incident. The tea and snack sellers at the stations where the train stopped were kept busy, although most travellers had brought their own parathas and pickle. Basant was happy with his young companions, and they were respectful to Tirath. Conversation, loud and rambling, ranged from the price of crops to the political situation. It was a nine-hour journey because of all the stops, one of which was Ambala, the largest junction in the Punjab, a huge station. Basant was amazed at the sight of so many people, all with somewhere to go. Then the train chugged out of the Punjab into the drier regions through Panipat and Karnal, and at last, in the evening Delhi station. Ambala was small compared to the station at Delhi.

'Look to your own baggage: take care of yourselves.' Tirath warned, 'there are pick-pockets around.'

Dodging and jostling their way out the five men hired a carriage, instructing the driver to take them to Karol Bagh. This was where most of the Punjabi migrant workers lived. The streets away from the station were not too busy, and soon they alighted at an open gate through which could be seen a courtyard with cool verandas, supported by pillars, that shaded the six rooms. Tirath's room was the middle one on the left; the other rooms were rented to workers from the Punjab two of whom had brought their families. A sleepless toddler playing in the corner veranda, although it was dark, stopped to watch the men unload their baggage and enter the courtyard; the youngster's mother rose from her low stool where she was breast-feeding her baby, lowered her veil and slipped into the corner room.

The men spoke quietly as Tirath opened the padlock and led them into his room. There was a portable mud-brick cooking fire with an iron handle. Beside it was a large tin of coal and pieces of wood. Two string beds, a small, steel trunk and a little cupboard with wire mesh doors for dishes and spices were the only furniture.

'Tea,' called Tirath, looking around at his companions, 'who can light a fire?'

'I will,' answered Basant, 'I'll take the fire into the veranda.'

'I'll bring out the coal for you,' Karam volunteered while his two mates, who were cousins, arranged the baggage in the room. Tirath opened a window that looked out to the side of the house to the wall of another identical to building alongside. From the trunk he took out two under-quilts, placing them on the beds and laying a sheet on each. A pillow on each and then he lay down, as an elder he was entitled to leave the work to the younger ones.

One of the cousins sat on the other bed and asked, 'Uncle, we have the address of a relative in Delhi. After tea we'll look him up.'

'It's late. You're welcome to wait till morning,' replied Tirath.

All four young men went out after tea; only Basant and Karam returned.

'Uncle, my cousins found their relative, a distant cousin. May I remain here with you? I feel at home with you and Basant.' Karam asked.

'Certainly, perhaps we'll borrow a bed from a neighbour in the courtyard.'

Tirath found work for Basant, less well paid than an experienced fully skilled man, but Basant would learn and be paid more in the future. The workshop belonged to a building firm who provided windows and doors to a contractor: these were assembled at the workshop, sometimes inside but often on the street, especially in winter to catch the heat of the sun. The surrounds and frames were constructed at the site. Basant began his days at the workshop but was often called out to the building site. He was amazed to see the tall four and five storey buildings taking shape: in the village most houses were ground level and a few had a first floor. At first he missed the closeness of the community in the village but soon he became used to the differences in the city. Many more vehicles, even some cars and trucks, people from all over India and the British. He didn't feel so out of place with his colouring though he was still conscious of it. He made friends with the other apprentices, or perhaps it was they who made the first approach, as Basant was his usual shy self with strangers. The young trainee carpenters were from all parts of India and spoke different languages but could make themselves understood with signs and a few words.

Tirath was pleased with Basant's progress and told him so. 'You've settled down well, I wouldn't want you to go somewhere else to work. I believe these British employers are fairer than our own people, in many ways,' Tirath said.

Basant followed his lead in his relationships with everyone at work. He couldn't make this amount of money in the village, and was satisfied for the present.

Karam found labouring work in one of the large shops in the Chandni Chowk, the famous Delhi bazaar, and in the evenings went in search of the Congress Party activists. He found the party were indeed preparing to make the British authorities aware of the anniversary of the First War of Independence. That night he recounted the day to Basant. 'The Congress is printing leaflets to be taken to every village in the Punjab. I helped to reword the message today, and I must recruit more volunteers. Can you help, Basant?'

'I am the only earner in my family so I must work, but when I have time, I will come and help.'

Once a week, on his day off, he would go to the gurdwara dedicated to the ninth guru, then to Karam's small political meetings although when they planned processions he refused to join them.

One Sunday, following a meeting, Karam said, 'I'm going to Chandni Chowk.'

'That's where you work.'

'I'm not going to work.'

'Do you have something to buy there?' Basant asked.

'Yes. In a way I do have something to buy. Want to come?'

Basant nodded and fell into the rhythm of Karam's strides. 'Will it take long?'

'That depends,' Karam turned to give Basant a smile.

When they came to the bazaar Karam hired a trap murmuring 'the red lane' to the driver.

'You've not been this way before,' he turned to Basant.

'I've only been as far as your workplace. What is that ... a mosque?'

'Yes, the Jama Masjid. Old and impressive.'

About a mile further, where the street turned north, the trap stopped. The two friends stepped off, Karam paid the driver, leading Basant into a lane on either side of which the shop fronts were not lined with shelves of wares to sell but were the rooms of a home with curtains, a bed, table and lamp, a red light. In each sat a scantily clad woman ready to beckon to whichever man in the street looked her way.

'Hmm. Obviously, you've been here before, Karam.'

'Obviously, I have.' Karam walked steadily past the shops.

'These women ...'

'... are selling their bodies. But we're not buying. Not from them. Keep walking.'

At the end of the lane there was a square, a space large enough for twenty coaches to manoeuvre easily. The buildings around had pillared verandas which led to stairs to the upper storeys of the buildings. Each level had deep balconies behind which were rooms full of light and music. Basant gasped as the whole place seemed a haven of entertainment.

'Come on.' Karam walked to the first entrance on his left.

A burly man with staff in hand blocked their path, 'Any weapons?'

'None,' answered Karam holding out his arms, nodding to Basant to do the same. They wore thin shirts and pyjamas with turbans on their heads, the hot summer had ended but it was still not cold enough to carry blankets. The man slid his hands down Karam's sides and along the inside of his legs, doing the same to Basant, nodding to another man who was in the shadows.

'It will be one rupee at the top,' he said.

A gate creaked open as Karam moved towards the shadows, climbing a staircase to the brightly lit first floor. Here there were doors of different colours to six small rooms which they passed to climb to the second floor. Two men sat at a table in the foyer. Karam paid the money, motioning Basant with a smile towards a half open door from where music mixed with the sound of anklet bells and a woman's bright and happy singing came.

They removed their shoes before entering and Basant was startled by the light and colour in the room, raising his arm to cover his eyes. The song had finished and there was a chorus of male voices shouting 'Vah, vah,' with arms stretched out towards the dancers.

Karam found them two spaces to sit amongst the audience of about twenty men who ranged from fifteen to fifty years of age. They sat alongside one wall on cushions while at the opposite side of the room to them, on a raised dais, were the male musicians, a tabla drum player and a hand-operated harmonium player. Sitting cross-legged with a fan in her left hand was the madam, resplendent in green and gold satin, hair piled high and pinned with jewels: the girls entered and exited through a door behind her. A murmur of excitement spread through the audience as the madam spoke the words, 'Is Sajida not ready yet? Don't keep us waiting girl!' She smiled conspiratorially at the men in front of her.

They heard her anklet bells first as she marked time to the beat of her song, the drum picked it up quietly, not to drown out the bells, first her foot, henna-printed, then her leg clothed in white satin; the harmonium joined in as she spun through the door and into the centre of the room, a vision in white with silver jewellery sparkling on her head, her face, her neck, her hands and wrists. The audience gasped an appreciative, 'Vah,' and little bags of coins were slid along the floor towards the madam. She gave a nod of approval to each donor. The girl in white danced like a gazelle and sang like a nightingale. Basant watched in mesmerised amazement.

'So, this is where you've been these past few Sundays?'

'You like it, too. I can see it from your face, your body and your breathing. You gasped too when she entered. The temptress Sajida.'

'She's stunning and a lovely singing voice too. Shhh,' Basant wanted to listen to the lyrics. Two men on his right, rising to leave the room, walked in front of him: he bent towards Karam to keep his eyes on the dancer whose words brought images of a child in a wood and the discoveries there, relating them to first love. She used all the space in the room, coming close to the audience who could reach out and touch her, though she always managed to swerve away, with a tantalising look at the last minute. And then the finale, she spun around and around, falling to the centre of the room in a graceful pile. Karam produced a small bag, reaching forward and sliding it towards her. She gave deep bows and made salaam to the men, walking backwards to the door she had entered ten minutes before. Basant thought there was a special look towards him, someone who was her own age. Karam nudged him to make him move to the entrance: he responded, thinking they were leaving. At the desk Basant watched as Karam nodded to the man and to a pile of coloured discs and handed over money. Basant thought, so this is where he's spending all his money. I'll need to talk to him. Karam was given two discs, a yellow and a brown, before he turned away to the stairs with his hand on Basant's arm.

On the first floor landing, they stopped outside the yellow door where Karam leaned down to whisper in Basant's ear, 'Leave this inside. See you in the square afterwards,' gave two sharp knocks on the door with his knuckles, before opening it and pushing his friend in. As the door closed behind him Basant blinked, to acclimatise his eyes to the subdued light in the room. He saw a curtained window on the opposite wall: a door leading to the next room on his left and a bed to his right from where a woman, in a long see-through chemise, rose to take the disc from his hand. She lifted a candle from the sideboard to her left and looked closely at his face. He could hear rhythmic thumping from the next room. Upstairs the music was beginning again. The woman was dark-skinned and slim. Looking away from her kohl-rimmed eyes he stared at the perfect globes of her breasts. She was his height, older and smelled of sweet rosewater.

'Young, with white hair and strange eyes? Have you always been this colour?'

Basant wanted to sound manly and brusque but his voice seemed to squeak, 'Yes, it's ...'

'Yes, I know, albino. I've seen it before, it varies with different people. Your first time?' Basant wished she hadn't smiled. He said nothing.

'Don't worry about it. You can take your turban off, if you like.'

'I'm not sure if ...'

'You've paid, so you do,' she put down the candle. 'Look in my eyes and give me your hand.' He'd never looked in a strange woman's eyes. Did she know that this was a first as well? Her hand closed his over her breast, her other hand went to the cord of his pyjamas. His breathing became short and irregular.

84

The thumping speeded up next door as she pulled him to the bed.

When she opened the door to let him out he'd thought so much time had passed, but the musicians upstairs were still playing the same song. A very dark-skinned, thick-set man stood in the shadows watching him. The man from the room next to him, the blue door, which was now ajar, brushed past him and clomped down the stairs. The yellow door was closed. Basant walked down to the square where he took deep breaths of fresh air, trying to make sense of the business of this place; the entertainment of men.

Karam came running up behind him, 'I suppose we should make a move for home now unless you want to try a woman from the shops in the lane?' He grinned mischievously.

'You'll be a poor man if this is what you do with your money. I'll pay you my share of the cost of tonight.'

'I've only been here twice before, I swear, Basant. Well, maybe three times,' he shrugged.

'C'mon let's find a carriage, or a trap will be cheaper.'

'Yes, sir,' mocked Karam.

They walked through the lane where now most of the shop fronts were curtained over.

'Busy night,' Karam commented, nodding to either side.

'I can see a carriage in the street ahead,' Basant led the way.

'A carriage all the way! Can we afford that, Basant?'

'I'll pay.'

In the carriage Karam asked, 'Right, when are we coming back?'

Basant looked in the other direction.

'Ah, you didn't enjoy it.'

'I did. It was an amazing experience and I should thank you. I don't think I know anyone, but you, who would have taken me there.'

'We're mates, yarh,' Karam smiled, he'd thought he'd blown it with the staid, boring Basant but it was alright, he was actually thanking him.

'It's terrible for those women. What a life.'

'Terrible? Did you see Sajida? Did she look unhappy? She dances and sings, brings enjoyment and happiness to many men. What's the problem?'

'They're selling themselves.'

'It's their job. I spend all day on labouring work in that vile shop. Maybe you like what to you do, but for me, that square at the end of the red lane, is my only bit of light relief. Those women are wonderful.'

'Most of them have been stolen from their families.'

'Some are born there and some, well yes they're kidnapped.'

'And that madam, squeezing every penny from men like you.'

'I'm just a little fish. I can only watch Sajida, the real men with money are the ones who will buy her personal services.'

'Buy her?'

'The madam, in her house, those big guards, the puny musicians, they're part of the business of raising and training the Sajidas of Delhi: her virginity, her first time, will be sold to the highest bidder. It'll be a fortune.'

'And after that, the one first time, what happens to Sajida?'

'She'll still be a dancer but if the first man doesn't care to keep supporting her then she might end up in the lane behind a curtain.'

'That's what's terrible. She's a girl, just like our sisters.'

'No, not at all like our sisters, you can't mention the two in the same breath.'

'If you're sister had been kidnapped, she could be a Sajida.'

'If that happened she wouldn't be my sister anymore. She'd be part of that world. She couldn't come back and be mine as well.'

'I felt sorry for them.'

'Was yours good?' Karam glanced at his friend who looked away but answered in the affirmative

'Very good. It'll be hard to keep away.'

'Ha! You're caught.' laughed Karam as he jumped out of the carriage at their house.

Winter followed autumn: one day in the spring, Karam declared, 'I'm leaving tomorrow.'

'Are you on your way to Calcutta then?' Basant tried to hide his surprise at this sudden decision.

'No, I'm returning to the Punjab: to Lahore, there's work to be done for the party.' Karam's look showed that he would not be dissuaded.

'You will end up in prison, if you're not beaten to death in the street by the police before that,' said Basant. 'I'm sorry to see you go, my friend.'

'I ... I know but ... I must do it,' murmured Karam, 'I feel too strongly that we are shackled by the British.'

'Shackled? That's not you speaking. It's party propaganda.' Basant's words fell on deaf ears: Karam packed his bag and left.

During the summer, processions and meetings were held throughout the Punjab. In Lahore riots broke out: Karam was imprisoned . On his release he took the first train from Lahore to Delhi. As it passed through Goraya Station he turned his head from the window in case he should be recognised. Arriving in Delhi he went straight to Basant's lodgings. It was an autumn evening and Basant had washed and eaten after the day's work. The rain had meant everyone was in their rooms watching the water rush down the gutters and along the drains. Voices were heard at the gate and a man's footsteps walked into the courtyard stopping at Tirath's room door. The thin figure took off his raincoat and shook it in the veranda.

'Karam? Is it really you, my friend?'

'Sat siri akal, Basant. Good to see you.'

'What have you done to yourself, you crazy fool,' Basant retorted, as they embraced. 'What a state, you're like a skeleton.'

Karam had lost a quarter of his body weight in four months but his eyes still shone with the old fire.

'You were right, brother Basant. I was flung into prison, a filthy place; the cowards of our community, those brutes of the native police beat me but I'm still alive and more determined than ever that we must get rid of the foreigners.' He gripped his fist and waved it in the air.

Basant almost cried at the sight of his friend, 'Welcome back. Mad as you ever were, Karam. I thought I was thin, but you are so skinny you're all bones. Here, sit down and eat these parathas to fatten you up.'

Karam laughed setting to work on a meal, 'Now you're talking,' he said.

Later Basant told him, 'I received a letter from your brother and I, well ... I did reply, but I didn't tell him you'd disappeared with the Congress, I pretended you'd gone to Calcutta.'

'Good. Thanks for the cover. I'm definitely heading for Calcutta because some of our Congress members are in prison there, and that's where I'm needed.'

'Karam, it's your family who need you. Shouldn't you be working for them?' advised Basant.

'What do you suggest? I'm listening.'

'Stay and work here in Delhi for a few months. Get your weight back to normal. Send some money to your mother. Then go to Calcutta and see what's going on there.'

'I'll sleep on it, and let you know what I think tomorrow. Can I share your bed?'

'Unless you want to sleep on the floor,' smiled Basant, stretching out on one side of his bed. Tirath was already asleep and snoring.

When Karam woke Basant had gone and it was full daylight. He decided he must have needed the extra sleep, and took his time washing and eating breakfast, but he couldn't remain idle for long. Soon he was walking into the centre of Delhi, to Chandni Chowk, to find his old Congress mates. The meeting place they had used previously was empty but he sauntered over to the tea shop where they sometimes gathered.

'I am Karam Singh. Do the Congress members still have tea here?' he asked the owner who sat at the front of the shop.

'Sat siri akal, sardar ji,' the man addressed him by the title for a turbaned Sikh, 'You're out, then?'

'What do you mean?'

'You can't hide the look of having been in prison. I remember you from the spring; a bright, healthy young man. Now you're like a starving wolf in winter.'

'It hasn't killed me. I'm not giving up,' Karam muttered glaring at him.

'It may be the death of you yet. What age are you – seventeen, eighteen?'

'I look young.'

'Take care, son. I'll let the other Congress-wale know you were here. They'll be around tonight.'

'Right, I'll come by in the evening.' He wanted to shake the tea shop owner's hand but he knew they might be watched so nodded gravely instead.

He returned through the busy street dodging horse-carriages, ox-carts and men and women carrying or pulling loads. Around Karol Bagh it was less busy. The street in front of the house was still not a tarmac road. He went into the room, pulling the portable fire into the veranda, lit it and put on a pot to make tea for Basant and Tirath. He'd tell them his decision when they came in from work.

'I've been thinking and I'll follow your advice, Basant. I'll find a job,' he told them when they had washed and were preparing the meal. 'Let me knead the dough for the chapattis.'

'There may be some labouring work at the factory. I can ask tomorrow,' offered Tirath.

'Thanks, uncle.' Karam sounded genuinely grateful.

Later while Karam went to the Congress tea-room, Basant and Tirath remained chatting to the other workers under the veranda. They were asleep when he returned. He spent the winter in Delhi sending some of his earnings to his mother, and keeping up with political developments. In the spring he announced that he had bought a train ticket for Calcutta and was leaving in a week.

'We knew this was coming. It's surprising that you've managed to stick around for so long,' Basant laughed.

'I'll write to you. You're a true friend, Basant.'

'What for? Sharing a bed with you? You kept me warm. In summer you'll sleep on the floor.' Basant tried to keep the parting light but he was very sad at Karam's departure.

'He's wasting his life. He'll be killed, or hung, for crimes against the state,' he confided to Tirath.

The next morning Basant received a letter from his uncle telling him that he should be returning home in the summer: he'd been away for almost two years.

That night he dreamed of the house and Takri was there, pulling her scarf over her head, glancing towards him with large kohl-lined eyes. He awoke thinking he had not looked at her face properly since they were married. She'd always pulled her dupatta half over her face. He was a stranger to her, not at all a husband.

Tirath decided not to apply for leave from work. 'I'll wait until you return, Basant. Then I'll take a trip home.'

CHAPTER SEVEN

Punjab 1908

Basant boarded the train for the Punjab at Delhi Station, early on a July morning. He had worked hard: his earnings were safely tucked into a travel pocket in the belt of his cotton trousers. Tirath had suggested buying some material to take back for his family, which he carried in a new cloth-bag. The train originated from Bombay, so was already full of travellers but he managed to find a seat beside a man accompanying two women and a child. With his bag stowed under the seat, Basant settled down.

'Where are you going?' asked the older of the two women.

'To Goraya Station in the Punjab,' he answered.

'We are going to Amritsar, so you'll leave the train before us.'

He chatted with his fellow-passengers, it stopped them staring at him. Twice he bought hot, sweet tea from the vendors who carried everything they needed in a basket on their heads, boarding the train at one stop and leaving at the next. Observing the other passengers provided some entertainment. He smiled as a young woman who stood her child up at the window bars to let him urinate out, only succeeded in splashing the face of the sleeping man in the opposite seat. Basant watched him wipe them away with his arm without opening his eyes. Two men played cards while the older women watched with distaste, from time to time tut-tutting their disapproval. Playing cards was as bad as gambling. Everyone knew about the devout king of the epic poem who had gambled away everything, including his brothers and wife: following the loss of his crown he'd spent years in slavery.

The countryside changed from dry and dusty to the lush, green fields of the Punjab, and then Basant's station arrived. Alighting with his bundle, he walked across the platform into the street to find a horse-carriage waiting for passengers to make the six-mile trip to Rurka. Two other men spoke to the driver, climbing into the back seat across from him.

'Aren't you Kashaula's son?' the driver asked.

'Yes I am. Basant Singh. Did you know my father?' They shook hands.

'I did, we worked together. That was many years ago, you would not have been born yet. You were on the Delhi train?'

'Yes, I've been working there.'

The man in the seat facing backwards started talking about cities where you could find work, and make your fortune: Karachi, Bombay, Calcutta, as well as Delhi. This allowed Basant to sit quiet, listen to the sounds of the horses' hooves, and gaze at the fields on either side. The leaves of the trees lining the road were turning to red, brown and yellow. In the cool of the late afternoon it was a fine homecoming, he was happier with his life than when he had left the village more than two years before.

Reaching Rurka he nodded at the owners of the shops in the bazaar as he passed, stopping to talk to a couple of them. At the Mansapuri lane he entered the Hindu temple to ring the bell, lay a coin at the feet of the deity and say a prayer. As he slipped on his shoes in the street again, a child greeted him, turning to run ahead to alert everyone in the lane. Each neighbour who was sitting on their threshold to catch the cool, evening breeze smiled a welcome: Basant stopped to say a few words to them all. Finally, he reached the door of his house with the children of the lane around him, to find his aunt waiting at his door with a small bowl of oil. He stopped as she poured oil on the door posts before he entered.

'Sat siri akal ji. I touch your feet, Taiji.'

'Live long, Basant.' She placed her hand on his head, as he bent to touch her feet. 'You look so grown up, now,' she said. 'You have a beard. My, my,' and embraced him.

Bhani also hugged him, but Takri only smiled, raising her folded hands, then moving away as soon as the first words of greeting were spoken. She had smoothed her veil from her forehead before smiling at him which surprised and delighted him.

'Your uncles are away at work,' his aunt continued.

'Yes, I received a letter from them.' Basant walked towards the room door to lay his bag down.

'Tell us all about Delhi, and your work. Takri, bring water and make tea.'

Takri knelt under the slatted ladder that they'd had installed with the money Basant sent, to pour water from the large, earthenware pot, giving it to Bhani to pass to him.

He commented on it while drinking the water. 'This is a strong safe stair now, easier to climb than the rungs we had before.'

Takri took her place near the cooking fire, beginning to prepare the evening meal, at the same time watching Basant and listening to his voice.

'Where is Easrie?' Basant asked.

'She's sleeping,' answered Bhani. 'Tomorrow morning you'll see how she's grown.'

After tea Basant visited the neighbours before he returned to have his evening meal. Bhani had taken Easrie to the rooftop to sleep with her. He was alone with Takri.

'Have you been well?' Basant asked her.

'Yes,' she answered, raising her dupatta over her head.

'You don't need to veil yourself from me,' he smiled.

'It's just a habit,' said Takri raising her head, her dupatta framing her face.

She hadn't looked closely at him before; his skin was very pale, his white eyebrows and lashes were a bit disconcerting, she had known a woman who had patches of white on a mainly brown skin. She wondered if he was this colour all over, but looked away blushing.

His aunt came through saying, 'Basant, you sleep in the courtyard and slide the bar over the adjoining door, as I won't be coming through till morning. Alright?' She turned, giving them both another smile, before barring the door from her side. They both knew what this meant but tried to continue as normal. Basant ate his meal while Takri cooked each chapatti and served him. Then he climbed the wooden stair to speak to Bhani, whose bed was pulled over to the far side of the roof, so she could be near her cousins. They talked quietly as on other rooftops, neighbours were already asleep. When he climbed down, Takri had cleaned up the cooking area, and placed the two woven rope beds in the courtyard, as the aunt had advised her the day before. They were made up with clean under-sheets, pillows and over-sheets. It was dark now, and the only light was from two small oil lamps in alcoves in the wall. He crouched on his haunches in the wet corner to relieve himself, throwing water after the urine to clean the gutter.

Lying down on the larger bed, he was glad to stretch himself after the long day of travelling. On completing her evening chores, Takri put out the lamps and lay down on the small bed. As their eyes became accustomed to the dark Basant turned on his side, and looked over to her. Takri lay on her back gazing up at the stars in the night sky. She was glad there was no moon; it would have lit up the courtyard in silver hues. They lay unmoving until the only sounds were the night insects, and the distant snoring of the family on the rooftop. Basant reached over, his hand touching Takri's arm then slowly he stroked her skin. She didn't stir until she felt the pull on her arm. Then she slid over and joined him on the big bed. His aunt had told her what was expected, but she remained crouching in a sitting position. He had to stroke, and press lightly on her shoulder to make her lie down. He removed his shorts thinking, I'm scared, and she must be too.

They lay close together for some time. Then he pulled the cord of her salwar, stroking her thighs until he felt her body relax. Spreading her legs, he turned over and lay between them. Their faces touched; her cheek felt moist; she was crying. Turning back onto his side he held her close. After a time he fell asleep; she listened to his steady breathing until she too slept.

The call of the village night watchman, 'Awaken, keep watch,' and the clatter of his stick on the door woke them both, and this time there were no tears, just a feeling of being held and of giving and receiving love. She almost cried out as he pushed and entered her and then it was over very quickly, and he still held her. They slept again, waking and making love twice more. Then it was almost dawn. She woke to the sound of knocking on the door from their aunt's house. Rising and unbarring the door, Takri said, 'Yes, Taiji, I'll be ready to go with you in a minute.' It was time for their usual morning walk to the fields. The women were always the first to go to the toilet in the fields, under cover of darkness.

This morning, whilst walking along, Taiji said, 'Give me the sheet you used last night, Takri. I will wash it because that is tradition. Are you alright?'

'Yes, Taiji,' Takri answered quietly and again was glad of the semi-dark. Being a woman was full of embarrassments.
After their return, through the morning twilight, she washed all over using water from the large bucket, began preparing breakfast of yoghurt and chapattis. Basant was already up, removing the sheets and pillows from the bed.

'Taiji said she must have the undersheet,' Takri said with her eyes lowered.

'Oh? I've rolled them up,' Basant replied.
The most difficult time had passed for both of them, the days continued with the usual household routines and looking after Easrie. As part of the roof was leaking, Basant made arrangements with Bhutta to help him with the repairs.

'The annual mela at Bhani's in-laws village takes place in two days. We should all go,' Basant announced one day.

Bhani was excited, for although her child-husband had died when she was eight she considered his parents part of her family, visiting them several times a year.

'I will wear a beige dupatta today. I am a widow and shouldn't wear a dark colour,' she said with authority.

'You don't have to be strict with yourself, Bhani. Deep colours suit you,' said Takri.

'I'm a widow. That can't be changed.'

'Of course it can,' Takri's voice was a whisper now, 'you can marry again. No-one would hold you to a child-marriage.' She leaned towards Bhani as if sharing a secret.

Her sister-in-law replied angrily, 'I'm happy with how we are: you are so keen to be rid of me.'

'You know I would keep you here forever, if it were my decision. But you could be a bride in your own house. Your brother-in-law ...'

'No. Stop it, Takri. I don't want to marry him.'

'That's fine by me. Don't be upset. What will Easrie wear to the mela?' Takri changed the subject.

She had heard Basant's aunts, and the neighbours, talking about Bhani's situation. Everyone thought she should be married so Takri tried to smooth the path for the fiery young woman by dropping a hint. If her best endeavours were met with such hostility, then it would be more sensible to keep quiet: she wished there was more she could do to help.

The next day, dressed in their best clothes, chattering and laughing, the three young people and Easrie climbed on to the carriage, the same one that Basant had travelled on the day he returned from Delhi. The driver had made an effort to decorate the sunshade over the passenger seat, and the horse had bells on its harness so the toddler was well entertained as she sat on Basant's knee at the front beside the driver. Bouncing to the clip clop of the horse's hooves she laughed, reaching with determination for the reins. Takri wore her dupatta folded twice around her head, and off her face, so she could see. As for Bhani, she did not need to cover her face, until she was in her in-laws' village. They chatted and giggled quietly, trying not to encroach on the conversation of the other couple on the carriage. Nearing the town that was hosting the mela they could see carriages, ox-drawn carts and horse riders arriving from all directions. Those walking towards the town were hurrying along, hoping not to miss any of the fun. Well before they stopped, the noise of the crowd, the snack-sellers and the music of the rides had reached their ears. The smiling faces made everyone's spirits rise. At first, the three of them walked around looking amazed at the hustle and bustle. Such a variety of snacks: they tried the samosas with sweet and sour sauce. Basant encouraged the girls to have a ride on the wooden big wheel that was driven by donkeys.

'It's like the water-wheel, except it raises people up into the air, instead of water out of the ground,' laughed Takri.

The two girls loved it, and then Basant tried a bigger ride. Takri thought he looked fine in spite of the people who turned and stared at his pale skin. Basant ignored those who pointed, he was used to that, but Takri felt like sticking her tongue out at them. Then they bumped into Bhani's brother-in-law.

'Hello Basant. I thought you might be here today. Good to see you all!' He wore a light blue shirt with a turban to match. He was slim, small in height, about the same as Bhani, with very dark skin and a wide smile.

'We've been so busy with eating, and the rides. Oh look, I must buy a windmill-toy for Easrie.' Basant moved through the crowd towards the man carrying the toys.

'We'll not be able to come to the house,' Bhani said, 'the driver will be waiting now but I'll visit next week: it'll be quieter then.'

'Right, I'll tell them at home,' her brother-in-law shouted as he disappeared into the throng.

They made their way to the road where the driver was waiting.

'It's been such an enjoyable day. We'll have lots to tell Taiji,' smiled Bhani.

'Your brother-in-law is a good man, Bhani. He will ma...' began Basant.

'Certainly not,' Bhani cried, 'Now, you're spoiling the day.'

'Don't be stupid. You can't remain a widow when he is willing ...'

'I won't talk about it. Stop, please,' implored Bhani.

On the return journey Easrie fell asleep to the rhythm of the horse's bells. At home the aunts and cousins were treated to some exciting accounts of the day, and everyone agreed it had been a successful outing.

All too soon Basant's leave came to an end; he left for Delhi again. The girls, Takri and Bhani, lived together, building a lasting friendship, keeping house and looking after Easrie under the attention of their elders. When it was known that Takri was pregnant, Basant's aunt informed her grandmother, and Dara declared that he would be willing to adopt the baby since Takri already had Easrie to look after. Takri knew a baby in her father's house would give her grandmother much joy so she went along with the plan. As was traditional, Takri returned to her father's home for her first confinement: when she went into labour, her grandmother and an experienced midwife sat with her. As the baby's head appeared, Takri was helped to sit on the edge of the bed. The baby boy was delivered into the hands of the midwife, who was ready with a bowl of water to bathe him.

'Congratulations. It's a boy! May you have many joyous days such as this,' she said to Takri, over the baby's first cries, as she poured water on the little body.

He was wrapped in a small blanket and laid beside his mother. Tara came in and squealed with delight at the sight of the baby, giving her sister a hug. Takri looked in wonder at her little boy, thinking that if he'd been a girl they wouldn't have been quite so happy. Then the midwife might have said, 'Well, better luck next time.' Her grandmother might have hung her head, and thought of the expense of another girl, instead of a boy. The words of the old songs expressed the same emotion – 'the grandfather hangs his head and thinks of saving for the new-born's wedding dowry.' But for the mother, giving birth was just the same, whatever the sex of the baby. She checked his colour and there were no patches. Not a trace of his father's problem, she thought.

'Takri, let the baby feed at your breast. He must learn, and you too. It's not always easy,' said the midwife.
Meanwhile grandmother asked Tara to help her with another special task. 'Help me, Tara. Open the door of the store room,' she said carrying a dish of what looked like a dark red pudding.

'It is very important that no-one knows the exact spot that we bury this,' she whispered, 'only you and I know and we speak of it to no-one. Do you understand me?' she paused and looked directly at Tara, who realising this was important, nodded, 'This is called the aull. This has been part of your sister and her baby before he was born. Some people would use it for evil purposes, for witchcraft and black magic. That's the reason for the secrecy.' Tara nodded again solemnly. She was pleased to be part of an important ritual. Her grandmother dug a hole and emptied the contents of the bowl into it. Then she covered it very carefully, smoothing it over to blend in with the surrounding mud floor.

Takri breast fed the little boy, who they called Munna, for three months, and then he was gradually weaned to cow's milk, as he was to remain in Mehatpur. Now that she had nursed the baby she resented not being asked about the decision to leave him: she knew it was too late. It seemed all power was in the hands of the elders: she would only be in a position to make decisions when she was older, when her children would look up to her.

The family in Rurka had made several visits during Takri's long stay with her grandmother but Basant had not been able to take leave from work. He was told of the arrangements for the baby to remain in Mehatpur, and he was happy with this; it was not unusual for children to live for years in their maternal grandmother's home. The baby was taken to Rurka to introduce him to the extended family. After an evening of celebration, he returned to Mehatpur in the morning with his grandfather leaving his mother with Bhani and Easrie.

Takri kept herself busy. Giving birth to a baby boy had elevated her standing amongst the women of the extended family and the neighbours, so she now had a wider circle of more friendly women. There was Basant's cousin's wife next door, the potter's daughter-in-law on the other side of the well, and over the rooftop was a new Muslim bride, Jenna, who would climb down the ladder to sit with them in Takri's courtyard. She supposed that they thought of her as a woman now. She didn't feel like a woman. A memory of open golden fields, blue sky, water flowing out of the water-wheel with the laughter of children all around, came to her mind. She had played hide and seek with Karam, somehow believing it would always be like that, she would always be close by. If she were of Karam's caste then perhaps she would have been going to the fields with his lunch, now. Silly to think that, she chided herself: they were from the same village, and couldn't marry even if they had been of the same caste. She was the wife of a carpenter and like the other wives remained in her house all day, sitting on the doorstep in summer and the flat roof in winter to chat with the neighbours being her only relief from the household chores. Anyway, Karam had left the village; she would never see him again. As she turned the handle of her spinning wheel, tears rolled down her cheeks.

'You're not quite a woman but you're not a little girl either,' retorted Bhani, 'can't you just accept your fate?' She saw that Takri was upset, and tried to console her, in her brusque fashion.

'It's not easy.' Takri sighed, surreptitiously wiping the tears. 'In this village, we are surrounded by houses owned by potters, and a few Muslim families, the children play in the lane or on the roof, but in Mehatpur the neighbours are mainly Jats. I spent a lot of time in the fields with their children. I miss the open air and the countryside.'

While Bhani rolled the cotton for spinning, Easrie tried to help. At the sound of voices in the lane she ran to the door. At four years of age her speech was not progressing normally, but there was no problem with her hearing

'It's the postman,' said Bhani, 'perhaps there's a letter from Basant.'

There was a rattle on the chain. Through the half-open door came the sound of someone clearing their throat before speaking, 'Ahem, ... eh, Bibiji a letter for you.'

'I'll go,' whispered Takri to Bhani. She pulled her dupatta over her face, as she moved to the door.

Holding Easrie's hand she asked, 'Will you read it for me, Bawuji?'

'Of course, I will be pleased to read it,' he said, proceeding to take his spectacles from his shirt pocket. He was one of the few in the village with spectacles, and was often asked to read letters usually because the recipients couldn't read but sometimes so people could watch the postman's performance of taking them out of his pocket, giving them a careful wipe and placing them on his nose.

Standing in the doorway, Takri listened to the clear voice. The letter began with the usual salutation, 'I, Basant Singh, am writing to you, Takri.'

The main message of this letter was that he wanted her to travel to Delhi, as there were now more families arriving in the area from the Punjab. He ended with 'You must send a letter to let me know of the date you will arrive. Sat siri akal to the reader of this letter, and to those who may be listening.' The ending was the expected one, letters were seldom read privately: it was considered polite to acknowledge all listeners. Takri thanked the postman, took the letter and began to think of her response. The next day she told Bhani, she wanted to go.

'Well, I have no wish to see the big city, so I will stay and take care of Easrie,' said Bhani, 'She is almost five now and looking after her is not a problem. It never was but the elders have to interfere.'

'I don't expect to be there very long.' Takri ignored the slight about not being needed and continued, 'I may become quite homesick.'

When she discussed the situation with Basant's aunt it was agreed she should go.

'Times have changed and going to Delhi by train is no problem. By the time you leave, your uncle will be here to take you to the station'

The week following the arrival of the letter, Takri donned her outdoor skirt and pulled her dupatta over her face to walk out of the house, alone in broad daylight for the first time, to the bazaar where the letter writer sat waiting for customers. He had spread a small mat in an alcove between two larger shops, and this was his place of business. His desk was a sloping-topped box with an ink-well in the top left hand corner. Placing it in the middle of the mat, he sat cross-legged behind it, spending the day waiting for customers like any shopkeeper. Takri arrived, placing herself on one side of the box-desk, at an appropriate distance from him, holding the front edge of her dupatta with one hand and peeping around it.

'Do you want a letter written, Bahu?' asked the letter writer addressing her by the title of daughter-in-law, looking away from her face with due respect.

'Yes, Bawuji. It is to go to Delhi. I have a letter that I wish to reply to, will you read it first?' She handed over the letter.

'Yes... Ah... M'mm. This is from Basant. Yes, yes. I see,' while reading he hummed and hawed which amused Takri. 'What is your reply?'

Once she'd told him of the dates and times of her travel arrangements to Delhi he took only a few minutes to write the reply sending a boy from the shop next door to the post office for her. That was easy, she thought as she walked home. Had it not been for her heavy six-yard skirt she might have skipped along.

During the preparation of three sets of salwar-kameez for herself and the sewing of two new pyjama trousers for Basant she tried to behave in a light-hearted way, though she knew she would miss everyone she was leaving behind. But living with Basant away from the confines of the house in the village was an opportunity not to be missed. They would certainly become

105

closer, or so she hoped. While cooking and cleaning she hummed the traditional dancing rhyme about the new bride whose lover is waiting but she has lost her way in her in-laws' multi-storied house: 'Oh whistle for me my love to let me know which room is yours.'

CHAPTER EIGHT

Delhi and Calcutta 1910-1911

Very early on a spring morning, a light drizzle had been falling since dawn creating puddles in the lane and the bazaar. Takri, in green satin, veiled by a muslin dupatta, with a black shawl over her shoulders walked behind Basant's elder uncle who, on reaching the crossroads, bought two places on a tanga going to Goraya, a journey of six miles. There were three other passengers, two young men who sat opposite them and one who sat up front with the driver. Takri kept her veil over her face. The light rain dampened down the dust, cleared the air; passengers and horse appreciated the ease in their breathing and how the weather lightened their spirits. The horse seemed anxious to be off by the way he snorted and shook his head. Even the birds in the tree under which the tanga was tethered must feel it, thought Takri they seemed to sing more cheerfully.

It was a busy morning, a variety of horse-drawn vehicles from the neighbouring towns were passing through. From the lane which led to the bazaar she heard a chorus of shouts and made out the name Chinta. Into view came two young men, one completely naked, except for his roughly tied turban, and leaning on the other; shuffling towards the ancient banyan tree, the communal meeting place. Everyone on the tanga turned with folded hands and lowered head, to acknowledge the holy man's presence, then on a cry of 'chal ve, chal' from the driver the horse leapt forward.

'To have the blessing of our own holy man, Chinta, before setting off is good,' the driver said. His passengers replied with nods and words of agreement.

In Goraya, once on the station platform the uncle looked around for anyone they knew. Two women sitting with their bundles of baggage agreed to look after Takri.

'We're going to Delhi, it's no problem. Wait with us. What's your name?'

'Thanks Auntie, my name is Takri,' she replied to the older woman, lifting her veil slightly and nodding to the younger.

When the train arrived there were only two minutes to board. Everyone stood ready as it pulled in and Takri thought it looked too overcrowded already.

'Quick, this is the carriage,' she heard uncle's voice behind her. He pushed her on to the train: she turned to grab her bundle from him.

'Sat siri akal, Taia-ji,' she called and saw his face briefly before women behind her pushed her into the train. Clutching her bundle, at the same time sliding her hand over her head to lift her dupatta, she pressed into the carriage looking for a place to sit. The passengers, all women with their children, as this was a women-only carriage, sat on long benches facing each other in cubicles of eight each, four on either side. There were smaller benches for pairs, facing each other, at the other side of the corridor.

A voice to her left said, 'You're a slim girl. Sit here. Move over, there's room,' to the others on the bench.

Takri nodded her thanks. The women who had agreed to look after her had also found spaces to sit, the 'auntie' negotiating for her to be allowed to sit near them. Other women were good natured, moving from seat to seat until all were settled. As she became used to the rhythm of the train, Takri began to feel the heat in the carriage, although all the windows were open. She folded her shawl, tucked her bundle under the seat and settled down to pass the journey. The parathas she had brought she ate with pickle, sharing one with the girl, who looked less afraid than she had done on the platform.

'I've never seen a train before,' she whispered between mouthfuls of food. 'It was frightening when it screeched into the station, like a threatening giant, noisy and dirty.'

'It was magnificent. What an adventure!' smiled Takri.

'Oh, if you say so - I suppose it is. This is good pickle. Did you make it yourself?'

'Yes. My grandmother taught me. It's really simple to make, lots of salt, that's the secret.'

'And don't touch it if you've got a period. That's what the oldies say, isn't it?' They giggled.

The older woman was talking to another group, 'This is my niece, soon to be married in Delhi. I'm worried about the tailors and the seamstresses who might charge high rates. I can't sew, you see, and I couldn't buy any material in Goraya, my husband hadn't sent me the money.'

Takri leaned over to interrupt, 'I can sew, auntie. I've sewn my own clothes and my husband's.'

'You don't say. Stand up, girl and let me see.' All eyes turned towards Takri as she stood to show off her emerald green salwar-kameez. The fit, the stitching and the hemming were scrutinised and praised.

109

The auntie was satisfied, 'That's it then, I'll come to you when I've bought the material, Takri.'

'I'll only charge the rates that we charge in the village, auntie, though I might need to hire a sewing machine.'

'Have you used one? Well, I am surprised.'

Takri proudly answered, 'Oh yes, there was one in my father's village. I learned to use it there.'

'But will the machine make my boobies lift up like yours,' shouted an older woman, causing loud laughter from all of them, 'that would be a miracle.'

'I'll come to you too,' said another woman, 'Your hand-stitching is beautifully fine. Where are you going to live?'

'Karol Bhag,' answered Takri as the train slowed down at another station, increasing the noise around them.

The tea sellers boarded, calling out 'Chai Garam!' Takri paid one anna for an earthenware cup of very sweet, hot tea which had to be drunk before the next stop to let the chai-wallah take them away when he left the train. Fruit, coconuts and popcorn were also sold by children, boys and girls, but she was not tempted by these. She felt sorry for the beggars who moved through the carriage. At home she would have put a bowl of flour into their bag, but here, there were older women who were giving a coin.

The countryside changed from fields growing sugar cane, wheat and vegetables, much like those around Rurka and Mehatpur, to drier ground where the lack of water obviously made growing crops difficult. Long before Delhi the parched land made her feel homesick, and apprehensive for the future. At Delhi Station she was fearful of the crowds. It was like stepping off the train into a river of people.

'Keep together,' the elder of Takri's companions called out, 'until we find our men.'

'Is the whole world here? How can a station be so big?' exclaimed the younger girl.

They placed their belongings on the platform and looked around. As the crowd thinned, Takri saw Basant walking towards them scanning the platform.

She raised her hand and called, 'Here!'

Spotting her, he waved, hastening towards the group.

'Is this your bundle?' he asked.

'Sat siri akal ji. Yes, this one.' She pointed, and then introduced the two women. They were not surprised at Basant's appearance because she had explained his condition to them, although the younger one looked afraid. Takri wished she could nudge her to stop her staring.

'Namaste son,' the elder answered, 'we have come from Goraya and my husband should have met us. His name is ...,' she touched her niece's arm. 'Tell him your uncle's name.'

'Oh ... his name is Om Parkash.'

'I'll wait with you,' offered Basant, 'he shouldn't be long. It's busy on the road.'

The girl kept staring until Takri pushed her and mouthed, 'Stop staring!'

Om Parkash arrived, shaking hands with Basant and said, 'I have seen you in the area where we live. Of course all the Punjabis in Delhi now live in Karol Bhag, so that's not surprising.'

'Yes, that's true,' agreed Basant, with a smile.

'I have hired one of the larger carriages. We can all go together. Come along, you're both welcome to join us.'

Takri looked from the carriage into the streets of Delhi. So many people, cycles, horse-drawn vehicles and even cars; it was another world from the village, and everyone was so well dressed. They alighted from the carriage at the house, where Basant had managed to rent the room next to Tirath's for himself and Takri. Of the six rooms surrounding the central courtyard, two were taken by single men, while the others housed families. The men were expected from work as it was late afternoon and almost dark; three children played in the courtyard. The pungent smells of burning fires and frying onions were in the air.

Basant showed Takri the fireplace. 'We'll use these cooking pots and implements for the time being. Then you can tell me what we need to buy. Tirath Uncle will eat with us.'

'Of course, I'll prepare a meal.'

The woman who lived across the courtyard hurried over to them.

'I cooked extra vegetables this afternoon because I knew you were coming and you'd be tired. Your uncle mentioned to my husband that you were arriving today.'

'Oh, you shouldn't have gone to so much trouble. I was going to cook,' Takri objected rather weakly.

'No, no. It's no trouble. You must be tired after the journey. If you wish, you can give me the flour that I've used for the chapattis. I'll bring over the vegetable curry,' she insisted.

Basant watched while Takri wiped over the wardrobe in their room: he was sure he'd cleaned it already. When Tirath arrived from work he was pleased that a meal was ready, and enjoyed being served by the young people.

'You don't need to wear the veil in the city,' he advised Takri but she felt it was rude to abandon it completely and didn't raise it above her eyes. At dusk, oil lamps were lit, with each family group retiring into their rooms. No-one stayed up late as everyone started the day before dawn. At last Basant and Takri could kiss, and make love in a room of their own, without fear of disturbing anyone, and try to make up for time lost during their separation. She wanted to tell him about their son, their niece and his sister, but decided all that could wait. This night was for them alone.

The next morning, Takri's life in Delhi began in earnest. She saw British people for the first time and marvelled at the differences between them and the Indians. Differences in colour, language and dress were obvious, but the British manner and attitude surprised her. She realized they were the rulers in the country she had thought was hers.

A letter arrived from Karam, and Basant read it to her after their evening meal. As soon as his name was mentioned Takri thought it couldn't be the same Karam, and her heart raced when she realised, it was her childhood friend. She had last seen him before the wedding; so much had happened since then. Her life was centred round new people in another village; she was a wife and mother. Yet at the mention of his name her mind awakened as if a spark had been ignited. She was sure her face would give her away, but as Basant was reading he didn't notice. She could admit to knowing Karam, because he was from her village but she had to be careful.

'I think he is right to fight the British. We should rule ourselves. Don't you think so?' she ventured.

'Yes, I agree with Karam,' answered Basant, 'But I cannot spend my life with the Congress Party. Apart from the fact I've got you and a family I don't really want to be involved in politics.'

Takri nodded grimly pressing her lips together and frowning. 'Perhaps it is because we are from the same village that Karam and I think the same. I have heard it said that people from the same village have similar traits,' she teased.

'Yes, the men of Mehatpur are certainly more politically active than those of Rurka. Why shouldn't the women also be?'

They smiled at each other and Basant put his arm around Takri, and drew her close. 'But you are married to a man from Rurka, and you should forget the ways of Mehatpur.'

Takri laughed softly and let the night take over wondering if her yearning for the fields of Mehatpur would ever cease, and if Karam felt the same.

During the next few months she began to enjoy life in the city.

'You are an expert,' said the neighbour, looking admiringly at Takri's hands as she cut material, 'who taught you?'

They were sitting on the ground in the courtyard while Takri cut out a shirt. She had borrowed a sewing machine, begun sewing clothes for the men and women in the house, and been paid for the work.

'My grandmother taught me. I learned everything I know from her.'

'What about your mother?'

'I don't remember her. She died when I was four. I had three sisters, but one of them has also died.'

'What a pity. Did you know the girls in Delhi go to school and learn reading as well as sewing?'

'Why do they need to read? The scribe, or the postman, does it for us in the village,' asked Takri.

'So they can be educated, of course. Have you never wanted to read?'

'I'd like to read the Holy Book, letters from my husband and I suppose it would be interesting to read the newspapers. I'm used to seeing others doing it.'

'You might end up reading all the time, instead of doing the housework. Then your husband would beat you, Takri,' laughed the neighbour. But the laughter stopped short of her eyes.

'I can't imagine my husband beating me. He's such a mild mannered man,' Takri replied.

'You're lucky. Mine hits me at the slightest chance, even when I haven't done anything. I'm used to it now. He used to be loving and kind, when we were first married but he hates me now.'

Takri changed the direction of the conversation with her answer. 'Letters from my sister-in-law and friends, I would like to be able to do that,' she looked down at her material feeling embarrassed at her neighbour's admission of abuse, knowing it was a reality for many women. Some women were even beaten by their husband's female relatives. It was an awkward subject for conversation, considered taboo, although everyone knew it was a common occurrence.

The neighbour realised Takri was uncomfortable, and continued, 'Being unable to read is not a problem. There's always someone else who can read a letter, and write a reply, even if you have to pay them. How long will it take you to sew the shirt?'

'It should be ready tomorrow.' Takri finished her cutting and the two women left the courtyard to return to their rooms.

Life changed when a letter came from a friend in Calcutta letting them know that Karam was in prison after a bomb had been thrown at the Viceroy during a parade. Basant finished reading the letter out to Takri, but afterwards sat silently staring at it in his hands.

'Do his family know about his political activities?' asked Takri. She tried to show appropriate concern for a neighbour, but her heart was beating too fast. She wished she could fly to Calcutta.

'No, they think he's there making a good living.'

'Then we are closer to him than they are,' pressed Takri, thinking fast. 'We must do something.'

'We are in Delhi, what can we can do?'

'He is from my village, and ... like a brother. I should ... visit him in prison?'

Basant laughed, 'He is in Calcutta, Takri. It is a two-day train journey.'

'If I go the authorities will know he has someone and his spirits will be lifted. I am willing. I could take the boy who sweeps the courtyard; pay him to accompany me, you would know I wasn't alone on the journey.'

'I like Karam, and want to help him, but what you are proposing is a big step. Let me sleep on it. We'll talk more tomorrow.'

Takri cleared up and went to bed. She and Basant made love, but tonight it was tiresome, a duty to perform. Karam was in her thoughts. She lay awake thinking of the past, of hide and seek through the lanes, the boys with their hoops and poles and the girls with their ragdolls. She thought of an imaginary future where Karam could be with her. She thought how stupid she was, and tried to sleep.

116

Next evening Basant began by trying to change her mind, 'The train journey is two days and two nights. Will you manage it alone? The boy may be with you, but you will have to look after him, as well as yourself.'

'Yes, I'm sure I'll manage although it will not be easy. To the neighbours here, I'll pretend I'm going to visit my cousin who is ill.'

'Karam is a special friend to me, and for that reason I think you should go, but promise me you will be very careful.'

Takri was delighted. The boy was hired, tickets bought and the following week she was on the train east. She had no idea about maps and could not know where Calcutta was, but it was the train's destination, and she was not afraid.

Passengers of all varieties, light-skinned and dark brown, well-dressed and in rough-sewn clothes were on this train. The cries of tea-sellers, coconut and fruit sellers contributed to the noise at the stations. She was sure there were more people in this part of the country than in the Punjab. The changing countryside was new, and yet familiar to her. It was still India. The people were darker-skinned: the language changed from Hindi to Bengali. At night she slept on the bench, whilst the boy for whom this was a great adventure, slept on the floor of the train beside her.

Arriving in Calcutta, to monsoon rain, Takri ran out of the station to the line of pony traps. She had Karam's address written on a piece of paper, but Basant had insisted that she commit it to memory. She repeated it to the Bengali driver who nodded, and she and the boy climbed on board resigned to their soaked clothes though enjoying the cool change in the weather. Alighting at the house where Karam rented rooms, she found Sodhi there to welcome her. Basant had sent him a telegram.

117

'I did not finish work until late so I couldn't meet you at the station.'

'Finding the house was quite easy.'

'You are very brave, travelling across India, Bhabi.' Sodhi used the title for elder brother's wife to show respect.

The next day she went to the prison with an interpreter, a young Bengali man who spoke only a smattering of Punjabi, but it was enough. The tiny barred windows in the austere red-brick building made her feel sorry for those who worked there, as well as for the prisoners incarcerated within it. To the gatekeeper she introduced herself as Karam Singh's sister.

'I have come from the Punjab to see my brother. I'll wait here until I can speak to him.' She sat on a bench for three hours before she was taken to a room, and told he would be brought to see her. Her servant boy followed her like a shadow. Karam, looking tired and pale, was led in by a guard who motioned him to sit at a small table. Takri was shocked at his loss of weight, his dirty appearance and torn clothes, but she could see his eyes looked bright when he saw her. He stumbled across, leaning forward on the table as if for support. She walked over to sit in the chair opposite him.

For a few minutes neither spoke as if to break the silence was to start a new beginning in their relationship. Karam half-smiled and marvelled that the pretty girl who had played with him in the fields, was now grown into a beautiful woman. He cursed his luck in being the wrong caste, living in the wrong village but had that not been the case he wouldn't have met her. How wonderful that she should be sitting in front of him.

Takri returned a look of dismay as tears came to her eyes. A memory of him striding through the lane came to her mind. A striking extrovert, loved by all, here he looked battered and worn, except for his eyes.

'Hmm ... when did you get here ... sister?' He'd been told who had come to visit although the guard had added, 'Looks too pretty to be a sister, more likely a lover. They'll hang you soon, so let me have her after you.' Karam had kicked out and glared with hate at the man, despite not knowing who was waiting.

'I came as soon as we received the letter about your imprisonment. How long will you be kept here?'

'They have no proof against me. I was only in the wrong place at the time of the bombing. The Congress will work to free me.'

She talked about his family in the village telling him they were all well. She even mentioned their neighbour's daughter who had given birth to a boy, and gone to live with her husband in Delhi.

He stared at her for a long time, finally breaking the silence by saying, 'Did you know, sister, that I fell in love with that girl?'

She shook her head, 'No, I didn't know, but perhaps she felt the same for you ... though ... what could be done in the circumstances?'

'Nothing, we are tied to our families and can have no choices for ourselves.' He raised his voice, but continued with more control, 'I'm sorry. You'll be afraid to come back.'

'I'll be here every day; if they don't let me see you, I'll wait.'

The guard moved forward to end the session.

Karam was optimistic about an early release but it was almost a year before the final hearing. Takri lived with Sodhi who wrote to Basant to let him know why she couldn't return to

Delhi. She made friends with the other Punjabi women who lived in the area, borrowed a sewing machine to sew their clothes, and visited Karam every day that she was allowed. Some days she sat waiting with the other hopeful visitors, but came away disappointed. Joining the Congress to collect signatures for petitions made her feel more useful. There were six prisoners and little hope for three, but since there was a chance for Karam she must stay and attend every court appearance, her letters to Basant repeated this; she hoped her husband would understand. She didn't say that she and Karam had renewed their love for each other.

The community of Punjabis in Calcutta supported any member who required help. Takri and Sodhi could have asked for aid from anyone, but she had brought some money and he was only too pleased to have her around to cook, wash clothes and be company for him and didn't expect help with the rent. She was an excellent organiser, and housework was easy for her. On the day the six prisoners were to appear in court, to hear the final verdict, Takri and Sodhi arrived when the courtroom was already full: they managed to squeeze in at the back. If she stood on tiptoe she could see through the spaces between the heads of the others standing at the back. Although she could not see Karam, Sodhi who was over six feet in height, told her what was going on. All six men were there in the dock and Takri remembered her conversation with Sodhi that morning.

'Karam's lawyer is a secret Congress sympathiser. The best that can happen is that Karam will be released today,' Sodhi had explained.

'And the worst, he could be sentenced to death? Is that so?' she'd asked.

Tight-lipped and frowning Sodhi had muttered his assent.

Takri was hot and exhausted when the judge delivered his verdict. She could just see the top of his wig, but could not understand the language he spoke. However, the twitch of a smile from Sodhi, and the pressure of his hand on her arm, told her it was good news for them, but not for the families of the three men found guilty, she could see from the faces around her. As the crowd moved out of the court-room into the veranda, Sodhi guided her to the side, away from where the people were leaving. Presently, the lawyers came out with the three released men. Members of the local Congress party were also there to help the ex-prisoners, until they were reconciled with their families. Sodhi and Takri pushed forward to meet Karam who looked drained but happy. The lawyers indicated to the police that these were indeed Karam's people. Holding his arms they walked on either side of him taking him slowly out of the court compound into the busy street. Takri thought she should be happy but she had to bite back tears. It would be months before Karam would resemble the same young man she knew in the village but it felt good to have an arm around him. They squeezed into a pony trap that took them back to their room.

The rest of the day was filled with visitors to see Karam who had so much to tell them about prison life and they about what had happened while he was inside, and what could be about to take place now he was out. It was almost midday when he awoke, having slept solidly for twelve hours after Sodhi had helped him to bed. He drank several tumblers of tea before he asked for the soup of rice and lentils Takri was cooking.

'This soup reminds me of when I was a boy. My mother always gave it to me, every time I had a temperature.'

'I used to eat with you. Your mother would make a giant potful,' Takri smiled.

'It's light and very nutritious,' said Sodhi, 'and reminds me of home too.'

'Well, now that I'm no longer in prison, we should head home. Basant will be pleased to have you back, Takri.'

'It's been ten months. We didn't think it would take this long when I set off.'

'After a few more days of rest we'll travel to Delhi,' said Karam, 'It's a busy city this year. In December the Viceroy is holding a darbar for King George to have the Maharajahs pay allegiance to the throne. There's at least one who's on the side of the Congress. That should cause a stir.'

As soon as Karam had regained a little of his strength they packed, said their goodbyes to the Punjabi community and boarded the train to Delhi. Takri enjoyed travelling with them, and the servant boy idolised them, hanging on their every word and laughing at their jokes. A continuous, light banter passed from one to the other, but there were some serious conversations.

'Bhabi, will you remain in Delhi now?' asked Sodhi.

'I will for a few months. I'd only been there for seven months when we received your letter.'

'You were very kind to come to Calcutta to help me,' said Karam. 'And Basant is part of that goodwill. He is a good man.' Karam broke the two conventions of not making eye contact, and of avoiding expression of gratitude.

She glanced at him, then looked out of the carriage window and sighed. There was no denying Basant's goodness, but he was unable to stir the emotion in her that Karam's nearness did. If this was love then it was double-edged, a destroyer as well as an inspiration. She knew that if she had encouraged him they could have disappeared, leaving Basant

122

alone, but that would certainly be a crime. Whether it was moral duty, or genuine love for Basant didn't matter to her, she could not leave him or hurt him. Her decision broke her heart, but she determined to stand by it.

They arrived in Delhi as the monsoon rains hit the city: it took twice as long to reach the house from the station as the streets were flooded in many places where the drains could not cope. As they entered the courtyard the three of them were already soaked. Takri had a key to the padlock and let the men into the room giving them towels from the wardrobe. Takri greeted the women, and went into the neighbour's room to change. Sodhi had lit the fire and put on a pot of water for tea while Takri took the servant boy to his home. By evening she had tidied up the room and cooked a meal. Sodhi went off to look around Delhi and Karam slept for a couple of hours. When he awoke, Takri came in from the veranda with some fresh brewed cardamom tea for him. As he took the metal glass, he grasped her other hand and pulled her towards him. She stepped back, shaking her head in response to his look of longing. Turning, she hurried out to the veranda hoping he had not seen the tears in her eyes.

Basant came home, was pleased to see everyone and commented on Karam's loss of weight.

'Each time you go away on your Congress work you come back a skeleton. I hope you'll settle down now.'

'My calling in life isn't conducive to settling down, you know that, Basant,' Karam grinned.

'This second stint behind prison walls hasn't changed you?' Basant raised his eyebrows in query but Karam only shrugged at him.

'The prison was bigger, the language different, but the treatment was the same.'

'Were you ever near to breaking, Karam?'

'The breaking point was always very close. Somehow, they ran out of time before I did.'

'Go home, Karam. Your mother is pining for you,' said Takri.

'Yes, you should and you need a wife to stop you thinking about politics,' Basant added.

Karam answered while gazing at the floor, 'You two were married young as a result of certain unfortunate circumstances. It's not the best road for everyone.'

'So you're not going home but staying in Delhi?'

'It's time I found a room of my own,' Karam sounded as if he'd made up his mind. 'Then I'll look for a job and meet up with the Congress, perhaps in that order. It's what I want to do.'

'I'm going home,' cut in Sodhi, 'I've had enough of being away from my green fields. I'm homesick.'

'I'd like to go to Rurka in the spring, in six months' said Takri, looking at Basant. He nodded.

CHAPTER NINE

Punjab 1912-1918

Basant accompanied Takri to Rurka, and then to Mehatpur to see his son for the first time. There was much rejoicing at their return. The extended family gathered to hear about the two years they had spent in Delhi. Both were careful not to mention Karam and Takri's time in Calcutta as this might filter back to Karam's family. Easrie and Munna had grown so much since they last saw them. He was two years old now, and was told that Basant and Takri were his parents but he was shy, and only knew Takri's father and grandmother as his family. Her younger sister had been married the year before.

'Don't worry, Takri. He will know you when he's older. You'll always be his mother,' Takri's grandmother insisted. 'It is a great privilege for us to have him. He is our joy.'

'Yes,' joined in Dara who had now retired from work, 'he is truly the light of our lives.'

Takri was pleased to hear their words but she felt isolated, as Easrie was now very attached to Bhani.

She immersed herself in household chores, in sewing and weaving in the summer and knitting in the winter months. Basant buried their savings in the back room and returned to work in Delhi. Another baby was due, and Takri let her thoughts dwell on keeping healthy for her next confinement. Her day consisted of rising early, while it was still dark, to go out to toilet in the fields with the other women, then cooking breakfast for Bhani, Easrie and herself. Bhani did some of the floor cleaning and the lifting of the beds.

Bhani lived a frugal life which is how she envisaged that a widow should, what she thought was expected of her. She visited her in-laws every few months, always walking to their village. Although she was happy on her own, the two families had other plans. Her uncle mentioned that they wanted her to be the wife of her brother-in-law; on their side, it was a source of shame to her in-laws that she should be living like a widow when there was a man in their family who could be her husband. However, at seventeen years of age Bhani was adamant that she was content with her life, and had no desire to be married.

'I wish you would change your mind, Bhani. Everyone wants the best for you,' Takri broached the subject cautiously.

'I thought you and I were happy living together, and all you want is to be rid of me.'

'No, I don't want that, I will miss you very much, but wouldn't it be good to have a family of your own?'

'You are my family. You, Basant, Easrie. Am I no support to you at all?'

'Of course you are, but some people would say I was using you like a servant.'

'Why do we have to do what other people want?'

'It's the way of the world, Bhani,' said Takri thinking how different life might have been if she could have married Karam. They could have followed the Congress together. She remembered the work in Calcutta, and if there hadn't been the worry about Karam, she would have been so happy there. The women seemed to have more freedom in the city than in the village; Bhani would have liked it there, but they didn't live in the city and the pressures from the parochial attitudes of this community were restrictive for women.

For a few months the elders of the families stopped discussion of marriage around Bhani, and the two young women thought it had all blown over. Even Takri believed they'd relented. Then Bhani's mother-in-law sent a message asking her to visit. Bhani, thinking it was a usual request, took the short-cut through the fields, an easy walk of about an hour. Fifteen minutes later her aunt and uncle also left, boarding the horse-carriage from the main road: they arrived there before her. As Bhani entered the house, her mother-in-law rose to meet her. When she saw her aunt and uncle there, she knew what was to happen. Standing in the veranda she heard the bolt on the main door behind her slide into place. It was a trap, and to create a scene now would be to shame all of these elders. Looking from one to the other she realised there was no point in fighting, and gave in. She felt as if her soul had flown from her body, and looked to the sky as if watching it evaporate: Bhani was no more. Her eyes showed a blank and unseeing gaze which had looked to the heavens for the last time: it was now fixed on the ground.

'It is for the best, Bhani. We know it is difficult for you and for your new husband.' said her uncle. Her aunt stood to embrace her, but Bhani's eyes wouldn't meet hers.

'You've all betrayed me,' she whispered into her aunt's ear. 'Leave me to my fate now.' She pulled her dupatta low over her face and neck.

According to the ceremony of widow remarriage, a small durree, a woven mat, was placed in the veranda and the bridegroom was directed to sit down on it. Bhani was led over, and seated beside her brother-in-law. A sheet was held high over them by the elders, and then slowly dropped, so the couple were completely covered. The elders sat nearby, everyone listening to prayers from a hymn book. After about ten minutes, the sheet was lifted, and placed around the couple's shoulders. They were given sweets to eat which were also distributed to the neighbours who visited to convey their good wishes, some of whom had sat on the edge of the rooftop watching the ceremony. During this time the couple sat still in the veranda. Bhani's relatives gave their blessings and left.

On their return in Rurka they announced to family and friends that Bhani was now married. They distributed sweets. Takri's friends Jenna and Durgee came to congratulate her, but found her weeping.

'She is only a few miles away. Don't cry Takri. You could not keep her here,' Jenna said.

'Yes, I know, but I will miss her. She is so much part of this house.'

'Girls are only passing spirits in their father's homes, all the traditional songs say that and we know it's true. We also left our birth-villages,' comforted Durgee.

Takri sent a letter to Basant about Bhani's marriage, knowing he wouldn't understand the sadness she felt: he thought Bhani should have been more accepting and less stubborn. His return letter only repeated that Takri would become used to not having her around, adding that he wouldn't take leave at the usual two year interval due to the war in Europe which was creating a lot of work. Takri decided to remain in Rurka rather than join Basant in Delhi. To keep her marriage safe she must avoid Karam: he was so often in Delhi. She took Easrie to her father's house to spend time with Munna.

That year Takri gave birth to her second child, but the baby girl only thrived for a few weeks before passing away in her mother's arms.

'Easrie, fetch Chacha's aunt. Say 'Baby' to her.'

'Be-be,' repeated Easrie in the dull tone that was her usual speaking voice; at nine years of age she had not grown out of her speech impediment. Takri believed she would never speak in proper sentences.

Taiji came into the front room, taking the little bundle from Takri, 'I'm so sorry ... such a short life. I'll bathe her and wrap her in a coloured cloth.' The uncle was away so she sent for a cousin to organise the baby's burial, as young children were not cremated.

'We didn't call her anything but Baby, Taiji,' said Takri. 'She didn't have a proper name.'

'There's always the chance that a child might not live long. We just never know. Don't cry. You will have other children, Takri.'

Several hours later, two men left the door of Basant's house, one carrying a small bundle in his arms, and there was no mistaking their purpose. People stepped into the shadows to make way for them for it was a common occurrence; the rate of infant mortality was high

'You are not the only mother who has a baby. At least you still have Easrie and Munna,' Taiji admonished.

Takri turned her face to the wall. After a few minutes her aunt motioned to Easrie, and the girl climbed on the bed putting her head on Takri's shoulder.

'Easrie doesn't understand what's happened. Takri, make something to eat. If you make rice pullao, I'll join you. No-one cooks rice like you do. Get up now, my child.'

There was food cooked in Taiji's house for her three children, but she thought it better for Takri if she looked after her child, Easrie. Takri tried not to cry. If only Bhani were there, but she refused to visit. She was pregnant, and could have returned to her childhood home, to Takri, for her confinement, but the forced wedding had changed her so much, she was sullen and withdrawn. Oh, why were they so cruel to the girls? Takri sighed. Little Easrie was nine now; the age at which Bhani had been widowed. What did she know of marriage and its end through a death? Takri couldn't bear to see the remote, unsmiling person that her sister-in-law had become. She cried for the loss of the forceful, confident, stubborn Bhani, as well as her own dead baby. Jenna came over the rooftop down the stair when she heard, cajoling Takri into taking care of Easrie.

Three months later Takri was sent a message by Bhani's in-laws. Her baby was a healthy girl but Bhani was seriously ill and asking for Takri.

Takri was sweeping the courtyard when the messenger rattled the chain on her door. He'd hardly repeated the words when Durgee rushed in behind him. He was a potter, Durgee's caste, from Bhani's village. On spotting him enter Takri's house, Durgee had left her water-pot at the well and hurried straight over. Everyone knew Bhani's confinement was near.

'Is it good news? No?' She could see from Takri's face, through the thin muslin veil that she had pulled over half her face when the messenger entered, it was not.

'The baby girl is fine, but Bhani isn't. I have to go, Durgee.'

'Give me that broom. Of course you must go.'

'Can you take her back?' Durgee turned to the potter.

'No, I have work in Rurka until evening.'

130

'I'll call up Jenna's husband. He has that new, fast pony-trap, he drives for hire. As long as he's not already left for the crossroads,.... Jenna-a, Oh Jenna-a,' Durgee climbed the stairs as fast as her short, stout legs could carry her six-month pregnant body, shouting at the top of her voice. As she reached the top of the wooden steps, Jenna had also climbed her own ladder, popping her head up as Durgee was almost on the flat roof.

'What is it, Durgee? Stop shouting, you can be heard a mile away, and I am not deaf.'

'Jenna, is your husband still in the house?'

'Yes, is Takri alright? Is it Easrie?'

'No, it's Bhani.'

The two young women met on the roof above Takri's front room, with a few minutes of nodding of heads, and of whispers, the transport for Takri was organised. Below, Takri had donned her outdoor skirt and shawl over her salwar-kameez while explaining to Easrie that she would be back quite soon. Durgee struggled down the slatted steps holding the wall, giving the news that Ali was on his way round to the bottom of the lane.

'Don't worry about Easrie. She'd like to keep me company, wouldn't you? I have a new baby donkey to show you, born last night. So cute ... come along. We'll walk you down the lane. Ali will be waiting there and Easrie can meet his new pony.'

'Thank you, Durgee,' Takri's eyes misted over.

'Don't speak of it. I'll be needing help in a few weeks, once my baby appears. What's there to thank!'

Takri stopped crying when the trap pulled away. It was really fast.

'Hold on, Bhabi,' Ali said, using the title for older brother's wife, 'this is one of the latest in horse vehicles.'

131

'We'll be there in minutes. It's quite exciting. Do you have a queue of people wanting to hire?'

'Young people. The elders are a bit afraid of it.'

'I'm afraid!'

'I'll slow down.'

Bhani's husband, hearing the trap arrive, came to the door of their courtyard. He was pale and unhappy. He motioned for Takri to enter, remaining outside to talk to Ali.

At the bedside in the back room two women relatives rose to move to the end of the bed. The room was lit from two tiny windows high up on the wall. Bhani was on her back hardly breathing, her eyes closed and the baby lay swaddled beside her.

'Bhani, it's Takri... I'm here,' Takri whispered. 'Your baby is so beautiful.'

'I wanted to see you. I'm sorry I kept away.' Bhani's voice was weak and strained: she opened her eyes.

'It's alright. We'll have lots of time now. You'll come to Rurka with me.'

But it was wishful thinking: Takri kept watch as Bhani slipped away, dying in the early morning. Her mother-in-law insisted on raising the baby herself. Takri returned home to be consoled by her friends and family.

During the four years of the First World War Basant only returned to Rurka twice, the first time after Bhani's death, and the second to Easrie's wedding. As family gathered to convey their condolences on his sister's passing, the conversation turned to the children who were growing up. A tentative proposal of marriage for Easrie was put to Basant. It was from the family Takri's older sister was married into, and was a suitable match.

'Well, a wedding in two or three years, when I'm next on leave, and then four or five years later we could send her the second time, the consummation. Yes, it's probably right to do that,' Basant said to Takri.

'The match is in our extended family, he's an only son and I think they've accepted her impediment,' she agreed. 'Yes, it'll be fine.'

Easrie didn't speak unless she had to, and then the sounds could only be understood by those who knew her. She wasn't embarrassed because she hardly ever met new people. Takri thought she had Bhani's forceful self-confidence, but worried that it was all a show; Easrie might crumble when faced with serious opposition, as Bhani had after her second-wedding ceremony.

'Women must be extra strong. Don't ever give up, Easrie,' Takri kept saying to the girl, hoping repetition would instil the message into her mind.

When the time came for Basant to leave, he told Takri, 'I'll visit your sister's village and give the boy a betrothal sagan. A pity my uncle is away. It's good to have an elder on these occasions.'

At the prospective in-laws home, to make sure of their response, he told the boy's parents, 'My niece has a small defect; she cannot pronounce words and remains quiet much of the time. Otherwise, as far as housework, sewing and spinning are concerned, she is very able.'

The boy's mother smiled in reply, 'I have only the one son, and if she can't speak, his wife will not have arguments with me. We'll make a happy family.'

Basant was satisfied with this answer so the engagement took place with the boy being given a rupee and a dried date, symbol of fertility.

Takri dug up the earthenware pot which contained their savings, counting out twenty silver rupees; she reburied the pot with Easrie watching her.

'I'll need some fresh mud to cover over this hole, Easrie. Bring it from outside.'

Wedding preparations began in earnest with the buying of an intricately carved tall wooden almirah which had an upper section for hanging clothes on pegs, and a lower part, with two deep drawers for bed linen. Then Takri began spinning and buying the items to fill the wardrobe. Easrie thought it was so exciting, all these things for her, and the crowning glory was that beautiful almirah ready to be taken with her when she went to her in-law's house. Only one other girl in the lane had been given such a thing. She was so lucky.

Takri was cynical of the bridal gift-giving. She thought they were bribes to trick girls into believing they were loved, that they wouldn't have been sent away, but their parents couldn't break the tradition. And that was so convenient. A magnificent collusion to keep women invisible and compliant; moving them away from all they held dear when they were at their most vulnerable. All her childhood friends were far away. Tears of anger, and of powerlessness slipped from Takri's eyes. Yet she was fortunate to have Jenna and Durgee. Takri's third child, a boy, was born in March 1916, and died within hours. Jenna and Durgee spent eleven days and nights supporting Takri.

Two years later, Basant arrived a month before the festivities for thirteen-year old Easrie's wedding ceremony were due to begin. He arranged the band, the cooks and the gurdwara for the overnight stay of the wedding party. The week of ceremonies began with the frying of flour sweets which Easrie, smiling at all this attention, gave everyone to sample. Then the women of the family and neighbours gathered for the maiyan, the cleansing with turmeric and oil, ceremony with the singing of the traditional songs.

Here is the bride
called in from playing
with the other girls.

'It's time you were married'
sing the women
rubbing turmeric and oil on her limbs.

Red bangles sliding
on her arms
henna patterns painted
on her palms
under the red canopy
the women seem so happy

She thinks, 'This is fun, isn't it? Why is Papa sad?'

He carries her to the ceremony.
She hears the wedding verses
Through the darkness of the veil.

Now she is married. Papa says, 'It's a game. Play it.'

Through the veil

they give her hugs of farewell.
She is carried towards a new life.

Easrie returned the next day, but she would not be a wife until her parents sent her off the second time to her in-laws. Takri and Basant had thought this would be in four years when Easrie would be seventeen but her mother-in-law hinted that it could be when she was thirteen: that it would be a help to her.

'Why did you not say so before the wedding?' asked Takri, appalled at the idea.

'She will be fourteen next year. That's not too young. Why do you object to my request?' asked her mother-in-law.

'In my opinion, she is too young.'

'You came to Rurka when you were twelve,' was the response.

'There was a reason for that: my sister had died. You are there to look after your family. Do you only want an extra pair of hands? She could be a mother in two years; but needs more support, hardly able to think like an adult and already a mother. That's what happened to me.'

'So you are not willing to send her next year?'

'No, I'm not willing.' Takri's tone was final.

'You would annul the marriage?'

'Yes, if you ask for her now. I believe Easrie is too young for the consummation of marriage and motherhood. As a community we have to stop doing this to the girls. It's not the best for them.'

Negotiations continued throughout the year, but the rift between the families widened. Before they had agreed to annul Easrie's marriage, fate took over and her young husband died of typhoid fever, leaving her widowed. Her dowry, including her almirah was returned. She cared for it and polished it with love and pride, stroking the patterned wood, and telling everyone it was hers, her dowry. Takri wondered if the stand she'd taken against the early end of childhood had been fair on Easrie. It hadn't changed the ways of the community, but perhaps in the long term change would come, must come.

CHAPTER TEN

Amritsar 1919

Takri was twenty-five in the first spring following the end of the First World War. Basant, home on two months leave, suggested they attend the Baisakhi festival in Amritsar.

'Perhaps our fortunes will change after a visit to Harmandir Sahib, the temple of God. We should have visited before now,' agreed Takri.

She continued in a whisper as Easrie was sitting on the steps in the sun with her embroidery, 'Although I pray every morning, I'm losing hope that my babies will survive. This last was the third, and with no reason.'

'While we are alive, we must hope.' Basant looked sad and weary. 'I received a letter from Karam: he's in Amritsar.'

'Why is he there? Political reasons, of course.'

'Gandhi has called a hartal, a business strike against the Rowlatt Act.'

'What's that?'

'The war in Europe is over, but the government insists on retaining laws to suppress so-called revolutionaries. Karam and others like him.'

'But Gandhi wants peaceful protest. I have heard the town crier say that.'

'There are those who cannot restrain themselves. We'll be at the Golden Temple, a place of worship and peace: it'll be safe.'

Takri left her spinning, leaning her wheel on the wall and went over to the kitchen area under the open wooden staircase to begin preparations for the evening meal. Her thoughts were full of her last meeting with Karam, such a mixture of emotions, joy and sadness. She couldn't tell Basant that two weeks earlier she'd gone to see Munna in her father's village. She was feeling very low, and who should walk into the house but Karam on a visit to her grandmother? Like a fresh summer breeze, taking over the whole space of the courtyard, lifting everyone's spirits. They all smiled.

'Sat siri akal, Maji,' he bent to touch the old lady's knee and receive her blessing, 'You are here, Takri? How good it is to see you. Where have the years gone since you were married? And this is ...?'

'Sat siri akal. This is my son, Munna.'

'You resemble your father, only the colour of your skin is different. He's my friend.'

'Sit down, and have some tea, son,' said her grandmother.

'No, Ma. This is a quick visit. I'm on my way to the well to keep the water-wheel turning. It's my duty today, tomorrow I'll be leaving.'

'So soon? You never stay long, and spend too long away.'

'There's so much to do. I'll be going now.'

Giving a smile to her grandmother, with a nod to Takri, he was gone. Like the much sought for breeze in the heat of summer there's never enough of him, Takri thought. An almost tangible pain in her chest made her believe that heartache was a definite phenomenon. And when it became too much to bear, was that when your heart broke? What could she do to make herself happier?

Half-an-hour later, she told her grandmother she was going to see a friend's mother during the afternoon siesta. Instead she walked out towards Karam's fields, finding him watching his oxen while they trudged around the well. Under the mango tree, she sat on a large rock, while he adjusted the straps which held the animals to the bar. The crops were high all around, and everyone was indoors to escape the heat. He had spotted her approaching as she turned the corner of the field of sugar cane. After a while he checked the flow of water to the channels, patted the oxen and sauntered towards her. His shirt sleeves were folded on his upper arm, and when he walked the chaddar, the loose sheet round his hips and legs, flapped.

She felt battered by the cares of life, lost babies and lack of attention. She wanted this man, knew he desired her. Respectability took everything; she felt she had gained very little from being dutiful. If her actions were so wrong, she would face the consequences. So when Karam looked into her eyes, took her hand, led her into the field-hut under the tree she followed willingly, not with enthusiasm, but a sweet resignation to fate, a surrender to desire. Their love-making was frantic, an attempt to make up for lost time. There was nothing to say, they had understood each other from childhood: their love had grown up with them, now it was time to let it take its course. The laws of tradition and society had kept them apart but they clung to each other with the force of conviction that they were right. It was the happiest and most fulfilling act of their lives, a melting into each other's bodies. Afterwards they lay together for a long time, listening to the water, the parakeets in the mango tree: willing time to stop and let them be together forever.

The flickering flame of her cooking fire brought her thoughts to the present as she slapped a chapatti on the hot griddle. It was a short fantasy, that afternoon of fire and love with Karam, now she must accept that her life was with Basant. This love has longevity and safety, there is duty and responsibility here that cannot be shunned, and these are human beings who cannot be abandoned.

'Come, dinner is ready, come to eat,' she called to Easrie and Basant.

Easrie rising from her embroidery said, 'Aah, ou oo!' and climbed the ladder to fetch Basant. Takri prepared each chapatti for them, as they sat beside her.

Sensing the sadness in her mood he asked, 'Are you alright?'

'Yes, I'm tired that's all,' she sighed as she put away her rolling pin.

'I have to meet someone in the bazaar. I'll be back before dark,' Basant washed his hands and left the house.

Takri ate while Easrie stirred the boiled milk, cooling it for the next day's yoghurt. Then Takri prepared the beds. She loved the night as it gave her a cloak to hide her eyes, her secret thoughts. Karam was in Amritsar, perhaps she would see him again: that would be good.

Hoping to spend the thirteenth of April, the festival of Baisakhi, in the Golden Temple, Takri and Basant collected their son Munna from Mehatpur, and after a few days of enjoying his company in Rurka, they set off for Amritsar. Easrie was excited. At fourteen her wedding ceremony and widowhood was just

141

another happening; it neither saddened nor heartened her. It was like a story she had been told on a dark summer night on the rooftop, someone else's story. The family travelled to Amritsar two days before Baisakhi; setting off early in the morning by horse carriage to Jalandhar, another from there to Batala and changing again for Amritsar. It was a holiday for everyone for the winter harvest was in: a well deserved break on the first day of the lunar month of Baisakh.

On arrival in the town, the family took a carriage to Karam's room. He had written to Basant to say he would not be using the room, but hoped to meet up with them at some point during the festival. The next morning they paid their respects at the Golden Temple. Basant tried to answer Munna's questions: at ten years of age he wanted to know everything. They left their shoes at the place reserved for footwear outside the entrance, following the line of visitors through the gate.

'Look, there is a sign that says cover your head. Easrie don't let your dupatta fall off.'

'Na Na-a.' She was offended that he imagined she would let that happen, smoothing her hand over her head with care, tucking her dupatta over her shoulder.

The buildings surrounding the Golden Temple were white and ornately decorated, with domes and windows in the Mughal architectural style. The flight of steps down from the western entrance hid the shrine from view until at last at the bottom, the devotee could take in the view of the gold covered room in the centre of the rectangle of blue water, around which were the white pillared verandas with the blue sky stretching high above them. Standing there in that peaceful enclosure, it was difficult to believe a busy city was only a flight of stairs away.

'It is built lower than the surrounding buildings to symbolise humility,' Basant told Easrie and Munna.

The children were impressed, keeping up a flow of questions while following the other visitors in a clockwise direction. Easrie's speech impediment was hardly noticed by the family who had grown to understand her perfectly well, but other people turned to look at her when she made sounds that for them were unintelligible. She waved her hands about to Munna as if explaining what Basant had said. Takri smiled at their happiness.

A woman said to her, 'What is wrong with your daughter?'

'She doesn't usually speak, but is so excited at being here she's being a bit loud.'

Easrie was embarrassed and tried to remain quieter, but couldn't.

'Chacha, why are there so many entrances?' asked Munna, who called Basant the title for younger uncle because Easrie called him that.

'There are four to show that all are welcome here, no matter from which direction or caste,' answered Basant. Verses from the Sikh Holy Book were being read at various small shrines in the verandas. Everyone made their way towards the causeway that led to the central shrine.

'Is it real gold on the dome and walls?' continued Munna.

'Yes, it's pure gold plate.'

They stopped to take a dip in the holy water of the tank.

Takri and Easrie went to the women's enclosure while Basant and Munna stripped to their under-shorts and dipped in the main body of water. They had brought a change of undergarments. Thus refreshed they continued on through the verandas, murmuring the name of God.

143

'It is holy water because it hears the words of the Guru and people's prayers,' Basant explained. Takri sat down to pray near the tree that grew there before the Sikhs made it their holiest shrine, before the city that grew around it and was named 'the pool of nectar'. The children and Basant joined her with the view of the golden shrine in front of them, the trunk to their left and the leafy branches above them. Little birds chirped and flitted from branch to branch.

'Have the birds built nests in the tree?'

'Ah, ah,' nodded Easrie with her hand on Munna's arm.

'Chachi, what is the story of this tree? It has its own copy of the holy book.'

Takri answered, 'I have told Easrie this story. Hasn't my grandmother told it to you, Munna? I heard it from her when I was young. You know, God helps us at different times: we call this the tree of 'the one who consoles us in times of sorrow'. The couple who found this pool were very unfortunate. The children settled down cross-legged to listen.

'In the seventeenth century, there was a king in this part of the world who wanted very much to have a son. He worshipped God, and donated alms to the poor in support of his wish. His queen gave birth to seven daughters. When the youngest was born, her father stopped believing in God, forbidding all worship in the temples of his lands. The people were very sad. The youngest princess, Rajni, spent her days with her grandmother who passed on to her an unshakeable belief in God.

One day the king asked Rajni, 'Who provides your food and shelter?' expecting her to say it was he, the king who was her provider, but she replied, 'All this is from God.' The king was very angry. To teach her a lesson he forced her to marry a man

144

who had been crippled from birth, who was only mobile using a small trolley which he propelled with his arms. Because the crippled man could not work, he was reduced to begging for his daily food.'

'Could the princess have said she wouldn't marry him, Chachi?' asked Munna as Easrie shook her head at him.

'No, she had to marry the man her father chose. All the family tried to stop the marriage, but the king would not change his decision.'

'Then what happened, Chachi?'

'The king turned Rajni and her husband out of the palace, so she tied a rope to pull the trolley, with her husband sitting in it, from village to village begging for food. The people knew what had happened: they were kind and sad for her. She slept on the ground instead of in a royal bed. One night her husband dreamed of a leafy bower where black crows flew into a pool and came out with white wings.'

'Was the water magic?'

'He thought it was a sign that would help him. So Rajni pulled him along in search of the Guru of the Sikhs, who lived in the area, to ask him what the dream meant. When they thought they were close, they met crowds of people walking past them in the other direction. The princess stopped a man to ask what was happening.

'Guru Amar Das has passed away. We have been to pay our respects.' Of course Rajni was dismayed, her quest was ruined.

'Why do you look sad, daughter?'

She told him, 'We were hoping to obtain an audience with Guru Amar Das to ask him the meaning of my husband's dream. But if ...,' her eyes filled with tears.

145

'Oh no, look at us, we are not grieving. The Guru's place has been filled by Guru Ram Das, he is the same soul. Go to the Guru, have faith and your wishes will be fulfilled.'

'Thank you, Baba,' said Rajni, wiping away her tears.

'Pray to the Guru like this; repeat after me *Dhan Guru Ram Das*. He will hear you.'

'Dhan Guru Ram Das, Dhan Guru Ram Das,' Rajni repeated placing the rope on her shoulder, pulling the trolley on which her husband sat with his hands folded in prayer.

There had been some rainfall, and the verges of the road were muddy. At one point Rajni strayed off the beaten track, and the trolley's wheels became stuck. She was having trouble freeing them.

A tall Sikh man, wearing white shirt and pyjama trousers with a white turban stopped on seeing her distress and came over, 'Let me help you, Bibi.'

He pulled the trolley to a dry part of the road, tightening the rope when he saw it was loosened.

'Thank you, sir. I am going to see Guru Ram Das to ask him to help my husband,' Rajni felt this man had a kindly, strangely knowing look. When he put his hand on her husband's shoulder he gazed into his eyes and said, 'I'm sure our Guru will help you. Don't give up, young man.'

Rajni was tired, and the day was coming to its end when she pulled the trolley over to some trees near a pool of clear water. Across the field they could see a cluster of houses.

'We can sleep here tonight. I'll beg for some food in that village.'

'Don't be too long,' her husband replied.

When she was gone he saw a black bird fly in to the pool, but when it flew out of the water it had white wings. It happened again, and believing this must be the pool of his dream the crippled man rolled his trolley into the pool. When Rajni returned, she saw a young man standing beside her husband's trolley.

'Where is my husband? I was only gone a short time. What have you done?'

'Look at me carefully, Rajni,' the young man laughed at her, 'listen to my voice. I am your husband.'

She recognised him. It was a miracle. Word soon spread of how the princess who pulled her husband in a trolley had found a cure for him. He was no longer a cripple: they could be found working in the Guru's kitchen. For Rajni realised, on reaching the presence of Guru Ram Das, that he was the man on the road who had touched her husband. How could that be? She did not know, but she had faith that the Guru had been helping to cure her husband from the time he'd touched him on the road to the dip in the pool.

The king, her father, hearing of the miracle realised he had wronged his daughter. He also paid homage to Guru Ram Das, and was reconciled with the princess. This is the first of many stories about the pool,' Takri smiled at Munna and Easrie.

'It's so much bigger now,' mused Munna. 'Lots of us can dip in it.'

'More and more people came, it had to be enlarged and these beautiful buildings built.

'All around Bibi Rajni's tree,' said Basant. 'Guru Ram Das built a dwelling here to begin with. His son, the fifth Guru, started the excavation of the tank.'

Easrie nodded vigorously and made sounds, trying to mouth the words.

'Yes, I know you like this story too,' said Munna. Easrie liked being with her cousin. He asked the most interesting questions and then Chachi told stories. It was good.

They completed their circumnavigation of the pool, bought a small bowl of sweet offering, and then took the causeway to reach the room under the golden dome where they paid their respects to the Holy Book, gave their sweet into the communal dish and, in cupped hands, accepted a small portion to eat.

'The sweet has reminded me I'm hungry,' said Basant, 'let's go to the dining hall.'

And there, the family took their places on the floor of the huge shed. Basant said, 'Only take as much food as you require. No waste.'

The mats for the diners were arranged in long lines. Volunteers were giving out wooden bowls into which dahl was poured. Another helper gave chapattis into folded hands and a hundred people ate together.

'This is fun; so many of us at one meal,' smiled Munna.

When they'd eaten, they rose, taking their bowls to the washing area.

'Everyone is busy helping.'

'Yes, Munna, this is what it is to be a Sikh.'

Takri told them, 'I am going to help in the kitchen.'

'We'll collect our shoes, and wait by the gate for you,' replied Basant.

They spent the evening with Karam who was his usual bright self. He became Munna and Easrie's favourite uncle in the space of a few hours.

'You haven't put on any weight, Karam. Do you even find time to eat?' Takri teased him.

'I eat enough for my needs. You'll remember that I've always been thin.'

The following morning, the thirteenth, Karam arrived with freshly cooked, orange jalebis oozing with sweetness, for them. Then he left saying, 'There's so much to do. I might catch up with you later.'

'He's always in a hurry,' muttered Basant to his retreating back. He'd begun to think perhaps it was not such a good idea to be in Amritsar at this time; the atmosphere in the streets seemed rather tense.

The family wore new clothes for the festival; pink cotton salwar-kameez costumes for Takri and Easrie with dupattas to match; white shirts and cotton trousers for Basant and Munna. Basant combed his long hair into a knot on the top of his head before draping his saffron-coloured turban around his head. Takri plaited Munna's hair and finished it off with a square of saffron cloth over his topknot. She tied her own long hair, black and shining, into a bun at the nape of her neck and Easrie's into one long plait. They ate breakfast of paratha and yoghurt at a roadside dhaba and walked to the Temple for morning prayers. The complex was even busier than on the previous day. After walking around the tank and along the walkway to the central shrine, they took time to sit quietly, in front of the Holy Book, under the shining golden dome at the centre of the cool, calm water. Even though hundreds of people in their festival clothes passed in front of them, it was as if they were alone listening to the reader's murmured words. But only for a short time, as the children were too excited at the prospect of rides at the fair to keep still. There was always a fair on festival days, and this one was in Amritsar.

'You promised we would go to the fair, Chacha.'

'Yes, and we will go, later in the afternoon. You must wait until then, Munna,' Basant smiled at his son who couldn't seem to keep still.

After communal lunch with the other temple visitors, Basant suggested they walk to the Jallianwala Bagh, a garden close by.

'It is a peaceful square and the children will be safe. It is in the traditional design, enclosed on all sides, with only one entrance and exit,' said Basant.

CHAPTER ELEVEN

Jallianwala Bhag 1919

They left the Temple making their way along the busy street with difficulty.

'I've never seen so many people,' shouted Munna, 'Watch out, Easrie!'

Easrie could hear very well, and was already safe from the horse-carriage.

'Ahaah, Haaha,' she answered. They knew she meant, 'I was alright, but it was close.'

Basant had to ask a shopkeeper if they had passed the lane but it was there, another four shops down the street: a narrow entrance to a long lane with walls of two storeys high on either side. The four of them could not walk abreast, so Basant and Munna led the way with Takri and Easrie following. On reaching the end the children ran into the garden, with Mannu exclaiming happily, 'You wouldn't know from the street that this place was here, Chacha.'

'No, it's quite secluded and there's plenty of space. Let's sit over there,' said Basant. It was under a tree, out of the sun.

'It may become busier as more people finish lunch at the gurdwara,' said Takri sitting cross-legged, and looking with interest at the groups of families who were dotted about the garden. Munna and Easrie went to look around. It was not much of a garden, rather a bare place, but quiet. The only interesting corner was the one with the well. There were some low walls in the other corner and people were sitting on, and in front, of them. More and more men entered the garden, gathering in the corner opposite the well. Raised voices could be heard now.

'There's a ban on meetings. They think they're only having a discussion but the British won't believe that,' said Basant.

'Is that Karam over there?'

'I'll have a look, and then we should go.'

'Yes, call the children on your way back.' Takri was also growing concerned.

Basant strode over to the crowd of men. Sure enough, what could be construed as a meeting was taking place. He saw Karam amongst the men who stood behind the speaker, but decided to leave, rather than speak to him.

An old man whispered as he passed, 'They're breaking the law, and it's risky with the city full of soldiers, and everyone already tense.'

Basant nodded, walking away in silence. As he crossed the garden towards Takri, he saw both children near the well, waved at Munna and called him to bring Easrie. Takri was standing up now, collecting their belongings.

'The garden isn't safe, anymore,' Basant said, 'time to go.'

And then they heard the TRAMP, TRAMP, TRAMP of soldier's boots at the entrance.

'Soldiers?' Takri's voice seemed too loud: she glanced around, becoming aware of the silence. Everyone was looking towards the narrow lane - the only exit.

The troops lined up along the wall, orders could be heard, sharp, loud and brief. The crowd realised that they were about to be shot, there was a backing away from the soldiers, though many people remained still in disbelief. When the firing began, the noise was deafening and terrifying. The crowd screamed, yelled and again pushed back, anywhere to get away. As bullets flew, Basant grabbed Takri around the waist pulling her into the people behind them. She was screaming, 'Mannu, Easrie,' her arms stretched towards the well. She tried to free herself from Basant, but men, women and children were now pushing into them in panic; some had fallen. Over the heads of the crowd Basant looked towards the well for his children, where was Karam?

But these were fleeting pictures in his mind, his arm was still around his wife, and he was trying to find safety. Takri still screamed hysterically. When he saw a small space in the throng behind them he twisted around, and punched her. She fell limp in his arms. He held her, and stood still in the space, until they were pushed to the ground. He could hardly breathe, he could hear firing, he felt a pain in his arm and lost consciousness.

There was weight pressing on him as he came round, and could hear the soldiers marching away. He took short breaths, trying to keep still. Then he heard shouting, a woman weeping loudly, sounds of dragging. Pushing with his back and arms, supporting himself on other unconscious or dead people, he blinked the dust away and looked over the square. Men and some women were pulling bodies away, and helping the injured. Around him, others were coming out of the pile. There was blood everywhere. The crying and screaming was growing louder as relatives were found dead or badly injured. He felt numb and in shock. For a while he could do nothing.

'Hey you! Get up. Don't just stare. You're needed,' someone was shouting.

153

Basant's arm was bleeding, but it was not too painful and it was easier to obey an order, so he rose to his feet, and then remembered that Takri was there under the bodies around him.

'Wait a minute,' he called, coughing, 'my wife.'

Moving quickly now, he pulled people into a sitting position not looking to see if they were breathing, but attempting to make sure air was reaching those underneath. He managed to clear a space round her and thank God, she was breathing. Pulling his turban from under her and lifting her over his shoulder, he carried her to a space, sat her up against a wall, and then looked towards the well. He knew what had happened: people had jumped in. He hardened his heart and mind, clenched them as he did his fists, and tried not to think. A man took his turban from his hand, tearing part of it to tie around his arm. The rest he wrapped around the pale young man's head. 'Help me, over by the west wall,' he said and Basant followed him. Karam came into view behind the well, limping: there was hope for the children.

Takri was sitting up and leaning against the east wall looking around in a daze: someone had given her water. She turned her head towards the corner where the well had been, now there were bodies all around it. She prayed aloud for her children to be alive. Bodies were being laid out all over the garden.

Basant shouted to her, 'Get up, Takri.'

On hearing him, a woman approached Takri and began rubbing her arms. 'Takri, that's your name, sister? You know, you look like my sister. Don't just sit here. Everyone must help. There must be a reason that God has spared us.'

'M- my children,' pleading, pointing to the well, Takri's eyes filled with tears, she kneeled to grab at the woman.

154

'Get up and look for them,' the woman urged, pulling Takri's arms, 'come on. It's no use sitting.'

Takri felt herself move like a puppet. She crawled at first, then stumbled, on weak legs, straight across to the well. Karam spotted her, and started limping towards her. Basant and another man were lifting a body at that moment. He saw Takri and Karam and held back. They were in each other's arms. It was obvious, how could he have denied to himself that she preferred Karam? How could he with his albinism compete? The shock and horror of the massacre were wearing down his defences. He allowed himself to think of the ways that God, or his kismet, had never been good to him. All of his family were now dead. The woman he loved, tears streamed down his face. He bent over, head and shoulders reaching for the ground and sank to his knees.

An old man stopped him from falling flat on his face, 'Make your heart big, my son. Don't despair. These are God's trials for us, and can only make us stronger. Say Waheguru, look forward, raise up your head.'

The sound of ordered, rhythmic running reached them as the Sikh-soldiers, the blue-coated super-fit guardians of the Temple, carrying only shields and spears, appeared in the lane in twos and spread out amongst the injured in the garden. They began helping, and the sound of their calls to God, to Waheguru, filled the air. Several of them began writing down the names of the dead and injured. Water and stretchers were called for. Takri remembered Basant who was still moving bodies and people into spaces, and went to give him some water which he took without looking at her, his hands shaking. She saw Karam bending over a body at the well, and rushed over, her heart beating a terrible rhythm. Everything blurred. She heard a scream while lifting the child's head to her breast. Someone was calling for Munna. Who was it? She was pulled away, but then through the haze she saw Easrie's face. Her beautiful girl's features distorted, and covered in dust. Give her to me. Who has done this to her? I'll kill them. Where are they? She felt herself being pulled away, a man held her, carried her to the wall, then a woman's voice, calling God. What else is there? Takri thought, only God. Water was poured into her mouth, and splashed on her face. She choked and coughed as a voice said, 'It is God's will. We are powerless in these evil times. Your children were called; it was their time.' Takri stopped crying abruptly, stared into space and remained staring. Women pulled her up, and gave her things to do. Like a machine she began following instructions. She heard a Sikh-soldier say, 'it is an atrocity: we will be avenged. Those who died here are martyrs.' Takri stared at the man whose eyes were wet with tears, but his determination glowed strong. 'Martyrs,' she nodded, mouthing the words, but no sound came from her lips. She felt stronger as if the Sikh-soldier's strength had flowed into her.

Karam left the garden to try and find a four wheeled horse cart, if possible. He knew they had to leave before the curfew came into force at dusk. It was not difficult to find one untended with the city in uproar: the horse looked strong and the cart had guard rails along the sides. He removed all identification marks from it, driving to his lodgings, taking all of the family's belongings and his own; he wouldn't return to Amritsar.

On his return, he ran into the garden, shouting for Basant to help, 'We must beat the curfew or we'll not get out of Amritsar. Hurry!'

Silently they carried the dead children along the lane into to the cart; he'd given a boy in the street a coin to guard it, with Takri stumbling along behind them. The last bodies were being taken out of the well as they left but Karam knew they would lie all night, with people sitting guard against the dogs and rats, for there would be no cremations until morning.

The two men took turns driving the cart through the night; no-one stopped them, the police who were enforcing the curfew let them pass when they saw the grim load they carried and heard the words, 'From Amritsar.'

At dawn they reached Goraya where they were recognised as they turned left, into the Rurka Road.

'Basant, brother? Is it you?'

'And what's this? What happened to you?'

'Bloody hell, the children! Jallianwala Bhag?'

No reply came from the cart, but a horseman raced ahead of them to Rurka. At the crossroads men stood waiting, followed the cart, as it trundled through the bazaar and stopped at the bottom of the lane of the Mansapuri temple. The news of their tragedy had spread throughout the village. Family and friends gathered round Basant and Takri: taking charge of caring for the bodies of their children. The Congress members of the village recognised one of their own in Karam, who gave them an account of the troubles in Amritsar, before bidding farewell to Basant and Takri, as best he could because of the weeping throng around their house, and disappeared.

The children's bodies were laid in the courtyard where the family and neighbours had gathered, many leaning over the parapet along the roof, others sitting on the steps leading up to it. The lane was filled with cries of shock and dismay: the total number of those killed at Jallianwala Bhag grew beyond the true

157

figure, as vows of revenge and appeals for justice were made to the village leaders.

Following the cremation of the children Basant and his uncle took their ashes to Hardwar on the River Ganges. They were met at the station by the record-keeper who held the death-registers of their family. He entered the names of children, and asked if there were younger siblings of the family to be added to the list.

With a cold stare Basant answered, 'There are no other children. My family is dead.'

When the ceremony of scattering the ashes on the Ganges was completed the two men returned to the railway station, where Basant told his uncle he was not returning to Rurka.

The Congress activists in the village worked hard to keep the villagers up-to-date with developments. There were newspapers published in the cities but most news in the village was passed by word of mouth or by the town crier. Anyone who read a newspaper found himself surrounded by interested people. Women would cross rooftops or walk to the end of their lanes when they heard the crier's drum. Takri's courtyard became the place for discussion because it was there that the results of the massacre had touched the village, there that the grieving had begun and there that anger was now vented.

'Gandhi has condemned the shooting and called for an enquiry.'

'He's the president of the Congress party. The British must listen to him.'

'He has no power; he's not allowed into the Punjab.'

'The British are afraid of what will happen if he goes to Amritsar.'

On another day, 'The Congress Party has started its own enquiry. We'll show these ferengis, these foreigners.'

And later, 'The governor Michael O'Dwyer and General Dyer who ordered the troops are to be returned to England in disgrace!'

'Takri, you're children are avenged.'

And later again, 'Tagore, who is a great Bengali writer, has returned his award to the British.'

'My husband said it was a great honour, a knighthood, but Tagore told them, since they had badly mistreated his countrymen, he had no desire for their accolade.'

'The riots have not been in vain.'

The women thought Takri was listening but she had other thoughts. Her last hours before Basant left for Hardwar had been like a nightmare.

'I do want to be with you,' she had pleaded.

'Oh! Is that the truth? No! Takri, admit it, there's someone else you've always wanted.' Basant's anger and aggression frightened her, 'I'm leaving and I won't be back.'

'I can't force you, but please come back. I'll be here waiting.'

'You and Karam, I should have seen it earlier.' The look he gave her was pure derision.

She shook her head.

They sat on mats in the room.

'Does Karam want to live with you? Is that why he's not married? He's waiting for you, Takri. Isn't he?'

'He would not hurt you. And neither would I. He's married to the Congress.'

'That's easy to say, but he would take you away if he could: he'll come for you when I leave. Next time I see him, I'll tell him he can have you.' He was waving his arms and shouting.

'I would never leave you,' she insisted quietly.

'Only because you pity me: yes and Karam pities me. Everyone in this village does too. Do you know what they say about you, the most beautiful woman for miles around and she's the albino's wife. How's that for kismet? The beauty and the freak!'

At that he broke down and wept inconsolably. He didn't speak to her again, and the next day he was gone with the children's ashes to Hardwar.

Takri despaired of ever being happy again and told Jenna that Basant had left after a quarrel, but she didn't mention Karam; she could never speak about Karam to anyone.

'Basant has lost so much. For a man his son is his family's future. He is angry with his fate, not with you,' Jenna told Takri. She had two boys of her own who were now ten and twelve years old. She felt Takri's loss as if it were her own. Everyone in the lane had loved Easrie who couldn't speak but had no difficulty communicating her love and kindness.

CHAPTER TWELVE

Jenna and Takri

Jenna said, 'In our community we have a pir, a holy man who gives advice on all sorts of troubles. He may be able to help you. Will you come with me?'

'Yes,' answered Takri, 'if you believe in him, perhaps he will help heal this rift with Basant and tell me why my babies don't live.'

It was a summer's morning when Takri and Jenna set off in the early dawn; by the middle of the day it would be too hot to go out in the sun. After an hour's walk they came to a wall enclosing some low, window-less mud-brick buildings. People were entering and leaving by the wooden gate which was at the end of a path to a green, wooden door. Jenna knew that the Baba always received visitors at that time. The door was open into the main room where he sat on a dais with many people already gathered in front of him, listening to his words. The two women made obeisance to him, finding a space at the front.

Some minutes later, when he gave them his full attention, Jenna said, 'Baba, my friend has lost three babies before they were a month old. How can we ensure her next child survives to become an adult?'

The holy man beckoned to Takri who rose and drew near to him, keeping her gaze lowered. He placed his hand on her head, closing his eyes for a few minutes.

'I feel much sadness in you,' he murmured, 'Heavy sorrow at present, but happiness in the future. He will return, daughter. The one you love will return, and you must give your baby into another's care for five years. This sacrifice will break the cycle of misfortune.'

On their way home Jenna said, 'I think his advice is good, but would you be able to give away your baby?'

'Well, Basant would have to agree. I am pregnant now, Jenna.'

'I'm willing to help in any way I can. You know that.'

'You're a true friend. Jenna,' smiled Takri.

Later that week she asked Basant's cousin to write a letter for her and explained the situation. No reply came. As the months passed with no word from Basant the seriousness of her situation began to have its effect on Takri. Anxiety and depression closed in on her mind, she could not rid herself of negative thoughts. I must have fallen pregnant the month before Basant returned, and that was when I was with Karam. What did I expect? I'm not an innocent girl. Did I think it was too early to fall pregnant after the last baby had died? The baby died in January, in March I went to Karam, Basant arrived a month later and we went to Amritsar on the 12th. Was I already pregnant when Basant returned? All I wanted was to be a little closer to Karam. Didn't I deserve a sliver of happiness, after years of being careful? She began talking to herself and weeping. Jenna climbed down the steps from the roof and sat with her but there were times Takri hardly knew she was there and other women began to notice. They accosted Jenna at her place in the bazaar.

'You'll always take her side, Jenna, but she's not in her right mind now,' Priya, the barber's daughter-in-law said in her squeaky voice. 'I bring her water from the well in the morning, otherwise she wouldn't have any. She won't go out.'

'She mutters to herself all day as if she's possessed. It's true. You know that Jenna,' Durgee said.

'She isn't mad, she's extremely unhappy. Any of us would be depressed after what has happened to her,' Jenna insisted. 'Aren't we all lucky to have our families intact? Don't stone her because she's less fortunate than you.'

'I heard her say, whose baby is it? What does she mean?' Durgee asked.

'She's so confused. It's because of her babies dying young, and then the massacre. She lost three children in four months,' Jenna pleaded.

'But could there be another man? Is that what she means?' prodded the sweeper woman, Niki, who had stopped work to take part in the conversation.

Jenna's control was slipping now, 'Have you seen a stranger enter her courtyard? You're up and down the lane, cleaning and lifting rubbish all day, Niki. What's wrong with you women? As if there was room in our cramped houses and narrow lanes to have secret love affairs without everyone knowing. There's hardly time and space to have sex with our own men. You can hear, in five other houses, the creaking of my bed, when my husband and I are at it. Who's crazy here? It's not Takri. I thought you cared about her?'

'Yes, I'd do anything for her but, everyone knows, she's the best looking woman in the village, you couldn't blame a man for falling for her and taking risks. Even if they haven't seen her face, the rumours of her beauty probably have most of the men in the village dreaming about her every night.'

163

'My husband says the washer man told him he dreams about having sex with the albino's wife.'

'Durgee! How could you repeat such a thing! That's stupid man-talk.'

'I suppose we're being envious,' said Niki.

'Speak for yourself. I'm happy with my looks,' Priya replied.

'Pity about your buckteeth!' fired Durgee.

'D'you think it was the postman?' Niki asked.

'That parcel of bones! Our Takri wouldn't let him near her.'

'Oh shut up, Durgee! I can't believe what I'm hearing,' shouted Jenna. 'Now you've had your bit of fun. Get yourselves together and start helping. We mustn't leave her alone, and we must talk to her, don't let her talk to herself. And don't put words in her mouth about other men or you'll answer to me. This is not funny. Put a rota together, Priya. And Niki, you make sure there's someone with Takri all day. Durgee find out gossip from the villages around Rurka and repeat it to Takri over and over again. I'll stay with her at night.'

The baby girl was born after a difficult labour. Jenna was there and was concerned for Takri's life that she hardly looked at the baby, apart from seeing that she was healthy. However, Takri had known from her first exhausted glance at the infant that she was Karam's child. Her features were too sharp, she was long limbed and her eyes were his, light brown tinged with green. Takri had known his sister and this child resembled her. If people in Rurka didn't guess then she could never show up in Mehatpur. It was the worst thing that could have happened in the circumstances. Basant hadn't responded to her letters, how could she present him with this baby when he did return? And

164

Karam was gone too. She couldn't look for him now that would throw suspicion on her and this baby.

'Are you in pain, Takri? What's wrong?' Jenna was concerned.

'I'm alright, Jenna, I'm just tired.'

Her mind was in turmoil. What could she do? The women around her had no reason to be suspicious so perhaps she could wait. But then she would become more attached to the baby. The holy man had said he would return, she was sure he meant Basant, not Karam, but it might be years before he came back, and it would be more difficult for her to reject an older child. And if she needed help from her father, she couldn't take this baby there. Babies often died, and no-one knew why or even asked how it happened.

When the midwife and Jenna left the room Basant's aunt stayed to help her, and thinking that Takri was unhappy because the baby wasn't a boy, tried to boost her spirits.

'Look, Takri she's such a beautiful baby. You'll have a son next time.'

Takri was distraught. A new mother was expected to remain on her bed for eleven days and inside the house for forty days after the birth so she had plenty of time to think. A few days later when the aunt was in her own house, Takri took the pillow, covering the baby's face with it. Her link with Karam had to be severed. She would always love him, but never succumb to the desire for him that had given her this result. Why had she been so stupid? This baby would have a dreadful life with people always pointing a finger, referring to her as a bastard.

Jenna came in, seeing what was happening, quickly pulled the cushion away from Takri, lifting the limp little body. She began rubbing the baby's chest and back.

'Takri, what were you doing? Have you gone mad?'

'She's gone? It's for the best,' Takri turned to the wall and wept.

Under Jenna's massage the baby gave a little cough. 'No. She's not gone. What were you doing?' Jenna was angry. These Sikhs she thought, so many of them don't want a daughter. She'd been sure Takri was different.

'Nothing. I wasn't doing anything.'

'You were. What's wrong with the baby? Tell me why you don't want her.'

'Telling ... won't help,' Takri sobbed.

'I will help, but I can't if I don't know the problem.' She continued looking at Takri, then gazed long and hard at the baby: the truth dawned on her, 'She's not Basant's, is she?'

Takri's silence confirmed her suspicion. Jenna walked up and down the small room comforting the baby on her shoulder and thinking.

'Were you forced - raped?'

Takri remained still and silent. Jenna, climbing on to the bed with the baby in her lap, whispered, 'If you're sure you don't want her, I'll help you. It will look like she died, but she'll have a life somewhere else. Will you let me do that?'

'Yes. I can't keep her, but I don't want her to die,' Takri agreed.

'Feed her.' Jenna returned the baby to her friend's arms.

'Did you think you were the only woman in the world this could happen to?' she hugged Takri. 'My naive friend, you know, we are only human, ruled by our emotions, some more than others. You're not alone.'

Takri looked gratefully at Jenna who continued, 'You cannot care for this baby, but I think I know someone who will. Do you love her father?'

'Yes. Oh, yes.'

'Then forget everything else and enjoy her for a short while. When she goes everyone in the village will think she didn't survive.'

A week later, a troupe of courtesans arrived at the village. Their coming had been much advertised and the male population, outwardly calm and behaving normally were counting their savings. The visitors included male musicians, guards, porters, cooks and labourers, but it was the ladies who were the celebrities. There was the madam who ruled like a queen, two exceptional and popular dancers who also sang, named Sajida and Nargis, four back-up dancers, six prostitutes who neither danced nor sang but were kept busy: plus all of their personal maids. They set up large, luxurious tents in the maidan, the open space used for meetings in Rurka. Men came from surrounding villages and paid to see the courtesans sing and dance, but few admitted to paying for sex with them though everyone knew that did happen.

One night, Jenna slipped out of the Mansapuri lane to visit an old acquaintance amongst the courtesans. Hindu and Sikh women like Takri, due to their caste status, were restricted in their movements around the village, but being a member of a perceived lower caste, Jenna was allowed to go where she wished. At the side entrance to the main entertainments tent when the music and dance was in full swing, she asked the guards for Sajida Begum, and gave her own name.

'I'll wait here.' Jenna stood in the shadow of the tent.

167

Five minutes later she was escorted through a maze of maroon and navy cloth corridors to a small room strewn with cushions over brightly coloured mats. Jenna could hear the music quite loudly and the anklet-bells of the dancers beating in time to the rhythm. As Jenna stood waiting, a cloth was lifted, revealing a beautiful woman dressed in lilac from head to foot, gold jewellery hanging from her neck and forehead: she was the famous courtesan Sajida. She tiptoed into the room, keeping her anklet bells silent with her light steps.

She embraced Jenna, 'Are you well, my dear?'

'We are all well and happy, dear Aunt, it's five years since I saw you last.'

'We wouldn't make the same money if we passed by too often,' smiled Sajida, 'and the wives would begin to hate us. This way we're a novelty.'

'I am pleased to see you again. I have a favour to ask of you ... perhaps it will help you as well?'

'What is the favour?'

'A baby girl, my friend's child, three weeks old. She will grow up to be lovely and clever, and make you proud. She's not wanted.'

'O-oh, a love child? Or too many girls in the family?'

'A love child, my friend is not married to the father.'

'On the night before we leave, bring her to the side entrance. I'm becoming an older dancer at nearly thirty years of age: it's time I raised my own little ones, for my old age,' her smile was a mix of sad and thoughtful. 'Yes, this will help me. I couldn't have taken a girl who'd been stolen as I was.'

The next day, Jenna told Takri, 'Your daughter will live. The lead courtesan, Sajida, that is not her name, they give them other identities: she is my father's sister who was kidnapped when she was a girl of ten. My grandfather traced the thieves to Delhi too late, she'd been sold to a madam who said she had been 'used' now and they should leave her or have their family name besmirched by her experience. He believed they would make an example of his daughter to deter others who might search for their lost girls, and he left her. Years later, she told me she knew he'd been there. She was being kept a prisoner and told she'd have been scarred before being given up, if he had not left her. She'd fought them but the man who first came to her didn't rape her, was kind in the circumstances, she was a prize for them and has made so much money in her twenty years with them. But there's no turning back to a respectable life for them, society doesn't accept them. The clever ones make a good living as independent, talented women especially if they're musical, and I know from my aunt, their community treasure their girls over their boys. It's not ideal but ...'

'She'll be alive in the world,' Takri agreed. 'God bless you, Jenna.'

A week later, before dawn, Jenna carried a closed basket on her head, over the roof to her house from Takri's, and out of her door to the maidan and the courtesans' tent where she gave the baby to Sajida.

'She has my eyes, Jenna. I'm so surprised. Won't you tell me a little about her parents?'

'Her father is a member of the Congress.'

'Hmm. Anti-government. Flits from place-to-place. Yes? What religion, caste?'

'Sikh farmers.'

'That's enough. She's mine now. I've been thinking of a name and seeing her I know it suits her. Nur Jehan, my little beauty of the world.'

169

'I must go. I will look for you in about five years again. Goodbye, dear Aunt.'

'Yes. No other communication. That's the best way.'

In the dark, just before dawn, the troupe left Rurka taking with them a new, precious, little addition.

Basant's aunt had been attending a wedding in her father's village. The neighbours were told the baby died during the night. Butta, the untouchable, was accompanied by Jenna's husband and they buried a small bundle near the cremation grounds, in the area reserved for children.

Jenna told Durgee, 'We must keep helping Takri. She won't pull through without us.'

They knew that there had been no letters from Basant, taking their spinning and embroidery, and encouraging other women to join them, to Takri's courtyard, they kept up conversations of village news and gossip. She was asked for advice on sewing, knitting and weaving, but she knew they were really trying to make her feel valued, as they had done for months now. The aunt was pleased with the activity around Takri, but being concerned about Basant's absence, asked her grandson Surain, who was an apprentice carpenter in the village to write to Tirath about Basant. Tirath let them know that Basant had left his lodgings and his employment seven months earlier, without leaving a forwarding address.

It was when Gandhi called for a boycott of all foreign cloth that Takri really took notice of village affairs again. The papers were posted on walls around the village. Fliers were given out to those who could read, for those who couldn't, the town crier, beating on his drum, shouted out the news. The villagers learned that Gandhi, as well as being an England-educated lawyer, was one of them. He wanted a better future for the poor people of India, for villagers like them and they believed in him.

'What does the paper say, Surain?' asked Takri.

'Did you hear the town crier, Chachi?' asked Surain.

'No, dear. I couldn't walk fast enough to the bottom of the lane. But the women said something about foreign cloth.'

'Yes, Chachi, the town crier said the same as this paper, that Gandhi says we should spin our own cotton not buy cloth made in the mills in England.'

'Gandhi always wears homespun, and he dresses in traditional clothes. I saw him at a rally in Delhi.'

'Did you see Jawaharlal Nehru too, Chachi?' asked Surain.

'Yes, he spoke as well: he looked smart.'

'His family have burned all their English clothes on a huge bonfire. Now they only wear khaddar homespun in the Indian style.'

'I think that's a good thing; if we don't want the British here, then we shouldn't wear their cloth.'

'The Congress in the village is planning a bonfire on Tuesday.'

'Well, I'll bring my suits. And I must start spinning if I'm to have any new ones.' She took down her spinning wheel, as Surain smiled in admiration at his politically minded aunt, the Congress supporter.

On Tuesday everyone who had decided to dispose of their foreign cloth walked to the maidan contributing to the bonfire in a patient line. It was a peaceful demonstration, but for Takri it felt like a new beginning. Burn the old, bring in the new. Looking at the flames she thought our leaders are clever, the simplest of us can relate to the cleansing ritual of fire. Now we

171

can believe the world we live in can be changed; the old rules are not necessarily binding and we can make it happen. She would wear khaddar homespun all her life.

When a nationwide strike was called, all shops in Rurka closed. Surain came in from checking out a deserted bazaar and holding a paper said, 'Listen Chachi, this is the news – it says, the King's son has come from England, and when he visited Nehru's home city of Allahabad, the strike meant that no-one was in the streets to greet him – the Congress turned it into a ghost-town and ignored royalty! Shabash! It must have been as dead as our bazaar is today.'

'The British won't like that,' replied Takri catching his excitement. 'Good.'

CHAPTER THIRTEEN

Karam 1919-1941

Karam, witnessing the punitive measures against the people of Amritsar instigated by General Dyer, with support from the Governor of the Punjab, could not follow Gandhi's non-violence policy: it was too slow. Although, after the subsequent official enquiry, both men were proved guilty of negligence in their duty to the Punjab, the young Sikh activists were not easily appeased.

In 1920 when Gandhi advocated spinning every day for male and female members of the Congress Party, Karam joined the Young Sikh League who wanted to see more action than talk, and resented stooping to what they saw as women's work. The peaceful resistance of the Congress Party was not for them. They caused disruption in the Punjab, and in Delhi it culminated in the throwing of a bomb into the hall of the Legislative Council, where a meeting of the main parties to discuss self-rule was convened. Bhagat Singh and two other Sikhs were arrested on the spot, gaining immortality as martyrs for this deed. They were hanged in Lahore jail, although Gandhi had led a campaign for clemency. Karam was close to being arrested, procured a passport in the name of Kamaljit Singh and travelled to England. Among the Sikhs in London, he'd been given a list before his departure from India, was Udham Singh who had been raised at the Sikh orphanage in Amritsar. He told Karam he was waiting

173

for a chance to avenge Jallianwala Bhag, by killing the former Governor of the Punjab.

'And anyone else who might be around him at the time. I'm hoping for a small massacre of my own.' He smiled with grim determination.

'I was at Jallianwala.' Karam told him. 'It changed everything: the call for independence from all sides became stronger after the shooting. The Young Sikh League came into being. We were successful in all types of sabotage, and then I had to leave them. I'll help you, if I can.'

Every day Karam was reminded of the shooting in the Bhag, the deafening sound of firing, the screams and the eerie silence of the cart ride in the night. His last words to the children that morning were happy ones; that was his one blessed memory. He was haunted by the thought that if the family had returned to Rurka the previous day, not staying overnight in Amritsar in his room, the children would still be alive, and Takri not the devastated woman he had last seen. He remembered how beautiful she was at his well. And now their love-making pervaded his dreams, even after twenty years. He would wake up, in a state of limbo between ecstasy and horror; remembering she was another man's wife, lie staring at a ceiling in England and wonder if she still lived.

The fourteenth of March 1940 was a date Karam would never forget. He arrived at Udham's Singh's lodgings to find him polishing a revolver.

He asked, 'Where did you get it, Udham?'

'I bought it from a man in a pub.'

'There was only one weapon? How will I help?'

174

'What's the sense in too many of us being involved? One gun will do the job.'

'What's your plan?' asked Karam.

'It might be sensible not to tell you everything, brother. You could be arrested by the police as a friend of mine. Although, I don't intend to run so they surely won't look for anyone else. On the table there, have a read of my diary.'

'March 15. Caxton Hall,' Karam whispered, 'I see, he'll be there.'

'Yes, Michael O'Dwyer, and a few others like him who have accumulated fortunes from keeping the people of India in poverty. I'm going to empty the barrel at them. Pity these bullets are not closer fitting.' He continued inspecting and polishing obsessively, as Karam brewed tea for them. Later, they sat in silence gazing into the embers of the dying coal fire. Karam stood up sighing deeply, admitting to himself that Udham Singh was right. There was nothing he could do to help, he should leave.

'I won't see you again, Udham Singh. Good Luck.' Karam slipped out into the foggy night, travelling on a train to Scotland when his friend opened fire on the meeting in the Caxton Hall. Only O'Dwyer was killed.

'Only one? I thought I could have taken more,' Udham Singh grumbled to the police when they arrested him. Karam read in the newspaper that he was hanged in Pentonville Prison, London, his body buried in the grounds.

In Glasgow, Karam found work at the Fairfield Shipyard, renting a room nearby in Govan Road. He had given up his turban and beard in India when he followed Bhagat Singh, as turbaned Sikhs were too easily identified. Wrapped up against the cold and fog, wearing a long coat and cap, he looked like the other men, only when he spoke English could anyone hear his Indian accent. Takri would only recognise him by his voice now. It amazed him, knowing that he would probably never see her again, he still thought of her every day. She was part of the memories of his fields, his oxen, and the village of his childhood, the happy days before he joined the National Congress Party and grew up. He could walk along grey drizzly streets and still conjure up his fields in his mind. He heard on the radio the Congress was pushing for the British to quit India now. Previously, it was the Sikhs who wanted them out; Gandhi started off only wanting more power for Indians. Now freedom was close, but it would be after this war. He would turn fifty this year, and all that was behind him; his life now was this grey city, among these brave working people, in a different struggle, the Second World War.

'A penny for your thoughts, Kami?'

'Oh, I was thinking about the war. I didn't hear you come in.'

'Supper's ready. Coming through to eat?'

It was Betty Flynn, his landlady and a bit more than that. They met when Karam had thought his wage-packet was short and went to the pay office where she worked as a clerk. After explaining how his wages were made up she noticed from the address that they lived in the same close; he was the quiet man who was Granny Gibb's lodger on the first floor. At the end of the day, she found herself waiting until the men of his group passed through the gates, and then she left the office to walk behind him, wondering if he would notice her. Near the close he looked around, slowing down to say, 'Hello, again,' which she thought was so gentlemanly. She was a pale, shy, rather fearful spinster who found this handsome stranger from India compelling: on his part, he liked her because she was less forward than other women. Most men went to the pub, or stood around the street corner smoking after work, but she knew he went to his room and read the papers: Granny Gibb had told her.

'We live in the same building,' he said.

'Yes. Are you happy here, Mr Singh?' she asked.

'Are you happy, Miss Flynn?' he countered with a twinkle in his eyes.

Disconcerted she murmured, 'I suppose so.'

'I suppose I am too,' he smiled, 'How is your father?'

He knew about her father? Granny Gibb had probably told him everything. She couldn't half talk, that woman.

'He's better than before. Thanks.' She nodded to him, and climbed the stairs to her flat with a warm feeling.

The next week she invited him to tea, her father had expressed a desire to meet the Indian who lived in the close.

'I know you don't go to the football match on a Saturday, Mr Singh, so I thought it would be a good time. My father was in India with a construction company in the thirties; he was a foreman. Says he met a lot of - eh - Sikhs where he worked. You're not – a Sikh, Mr Singh, are you?'

'Yes, I am. I will be happy to come to tea on Saturday. Thank you.'

Betty was surprised at how much she looked forward to Saturday, and the visit. All the tension she felt with other men wasn't there with him. Kami, as his mates at the shipyard called him, accepted her situation, was kind and undemanding of her.

'How do you do, sir?' Karam shook hands with the thin, elderly man in the armchair.

'Hello, Hello. Sit down, near the fire. It's a terrible day outside. This rain is depressing. How do you find this weather, Kami? May I call you that?'

'Yes, of course, sir. The weather is damp in this part of the world, but I'm becoming used to it.'

After that first visit, Saturday afternoons together became a regular meeting time for the three friends. The theatre of war seemed far away, except when the air raid sirens sounded. Then, people went into bunkers built in the backyards, or to relations who lived in ground floor flats. Her father wanted Betty to leave their second floor flat, but she didn't want to go without him. When Karam joined them he helped by supporting her father on the landings, and carrying him down the stairs where they would shelter in the close, until the all-clear.

'You'll do yourself an injury, with my weight, Kami.'

'Can't leave you there by yourself, sir,' answered Karam, 'You're not heavy.'

Neighbours from the two flats above also gathered in the close mouth. The worst night was in March, when a parachute landmine landed on a nearby building bringing down a flurry of white flakes from the white-washed ceiling onto the group. But they were lucky; three tenements were destroyed that night and over sixty people killed. After that, it seemed more sensible for Karam to eat with Betty and her father every night, in case of another air-raid. After the meal, they would listen to the news on the radio. One evening the conversation turned to their memories of India.

'I went to Delhi in 1920, Kami. I took the job because I thought it would be something different to do. Betty kept her mother company while I was away, and we needed the money. I didn't mind the heat, and I wasn't too high-up a white man, a

178

gora, so I made friends with the local chaps quite easily. I remember this albino chap, a Sikh, a carpenter by trade. I'd not known about albinos until then.'

Karam tried not to show more than ordinary interest, but every muscle in his body became taut. He sat up in his chair, he had not expected this - the ghostly white face of Basant seemed to float across the twenty-one years since that night cart-ride. Karam looked sideways as if to see his friend, as he'd done that night, almost moving his hand to give him the horse's reins for his shift of driving. Betty noticed his unease, and his twitching hand, as her father continued. 'It was only a shock when you first met him, after that you quickly got used to the strangeness of his colour. It was unnaturally white, and so was his hair, his eyes too were flecked with pink.'

'Skin disorders are quite common in India,' added Karam, after clearing his throat.

'That's right, but I had never met anyone like him: I became very fond of him. Good worker, reliable and kind to everyone. He soon left because he was mentally ill. I found out later his children had been killed at Jallianwala Bhag.'

Betty added, 'I remember reading about that in the papers. There was a collection in England for the General when he returned. Dyer, I think he was called.

Karam's memories of the Bhag started replaying in his mind. He had no wish to share them with the Flynns.

Betty's father was speaking, 'I'm trying to remember the carpenter's name. I thought it inappropriate for him - it was … you'll know the word for the colour saffron? What's the word for saffron, Kami?'

'Basantee.' Again Karam cleared his throat, staring steadily at the floor with his hands holding his arms at his side.

179

'Yes, Basant! That was his name, Basant Singh. Anyway, we didn't see him again for nearly four years. I thought he'd gone to his home but he told us he'd been living at Gandhi's ashram.'

'Gandhi came to London when you were still in India, Father.'

'Yes, a very influential man, in an eccentric fashion. Don't you think, Kami?'

'I agree, but I wonder if India might have gained Independence before the war without him. He often delayed action.'

'Could be, people loved him in Delhi though. As for Basant, this albino chap, he came back to the company, we always needed good workers, but just before I left India for good, in '36, he was involved in an accident. Lost his sight, though I think his condition contributed to it, as well. It was a tragedy for him and his family. I explained that the company could give him severance pay as a regular pension or a lump sum. Which would he prefer? He said he had a daughter, and would prefer the lump sum: to invest for her wedding. Wise choice, I thought. I was not very well at the time myself, returned to Scotland soon after.'

Later in his room, Karam stared into the remains of the coal fire, letting his memories turn from scene to scene, like a silent film; to his days with Takri, with Basant, and the three of them together. The children's deaths were his fault: he should have sent them back to Rurka since he knew the danger that was brewing in Amritsar. If only... he fell asleep in the chair dreaming of the click, click of the water wheel, the slow circular motion of the oxen, the swish of water in the channels and Takri in his arms.

PART TWO

CHAPTER ONE

Basant 1919-1930

Basant tried to settle down in Delhi but his heart and mind were seriously disturbed. He blamed himself for his children's deaths. Why hadn't he taken Munna to the fair as the child had wanted? His decision had ruined their lives. He had heard that Gandhi's ashram was a place that welcomed those who wished to live like him, a simple way of life following the dictum that God is Truth. Basant thought that, as the Sikh greeting Sat siri akal meant God is Truth the Gandhian way wouldn't be difficult. In addition, he knew he needed peace and simplicity. He tendered his resignation, boarded a train to Ahmadabad in Gujarat, and walked from the station to the ashram, a group of low white-washed huts in a grove of trees, on the banks of the Sabarmati. Between the huts and the river was a flat piece of raised ground where about fifty men, women and children sat, singing hymns. Basant washed at a pump and joined the group. Although these were Hindu prayers Basant knew them, for he had grown up near a temple, these sounds had filled the air around his home each evening. Afterwards, Basant was given parshad, a sweet food for communal sharing. Gandhi was not present at the service: Basant knew that he was busy in Delhi dealing with the findings of the enquiry into the Jallianwala Bhag massacre. While spreading a sheet under a tree to sleep, he regretted not being educated and able to help Gandhi but he would do whatever he could in the ashram. It was a warm night, he placed his mat on the ground and slept.

Next morning, a young man approached him, joined his palms in namaste, and spoke first in Gujarati, then in English. Basant had picked up some English from working in Delhi, and from this, combined with the youth's gestures he understood that he was invited to the huts. He nodded in agreement, but took his time watching the morning unfold around the compound. The youth who had spoken to him was repairing a broken fence. Basant observed his efforts for a few minutes, then tied up his bundle, and went to help. Those looking on soon knew that a skilled wood-worker was amongst them, for the fence was soon up. As he hammered in the last post a child took his hand, leading him to the veranda where an old woman, whom the child called Ba, gave him a bowl of washed, sliced fruit. Many others, who joined the ashram like Basant, had never met Gandhi or his wife, but soon began calling them Bapuji and Ba, father and mother.

About a month later, early in the evening Basant heard the children's voices, happy and excited, in a louder than usual commotion. Before he could leave the work he was engaged in, sharpening tools, a child ran into the hut and taking his hand tried to pull him up. Basant pretended to be surprised, allowing himself to be led outside. There in the middle of the yard, with the throng of laughing children around him stood a thin man wearing the traditional Hindu garment, the dhoti, with round spectacles on his large pointed nose and a huge infectious grin that almost stretched from ear to ear. It could only have been Mohandas Gandhi. Basant felt awed in the presence of this famous man, who had fought discrimination in South Africa, was now one of India's leaders: a man with no property or savings, but with much power and prestige.

The child who was pulling Basant along stopped in front of Gandhi, shouting above the other voices, 'Look, Bapuji, you went to the Punjab, and sent us a Sikh!'

'He is our friend,' added another. 'He carves toys for us.'

'I'm afraid it was not I who sent your friend. It must have been God,' said Gandhi, 'but I am pleased to meet him.'

'His name is Basant Singh,' the first child said, as Basant bent to touch Gandhi's feet.

'Welcome, Basant. Be blessed with long life,' the great man said.

Everyone in the ashram followed Gandhi's example of completing a fair share of the daily chores. One morning, Basant and Gandhi sat together in the kitchen peeling potatoes.

'Basant, look, there is my wife,' said Gandhi. He spoke in a mixture of Hindi and Gujarati, with gestures to help.

Basant nodded, 'Yes. Ba is your wife.'

'What about your wife, Basant? Where is she?' Gandhi asked.

'In Punjab,' replied Basant.

'Why are you not with her?' asked Gandhi looking directly into Basant's eyes. He had realised that the quiet, unnaturally pale Punjabi who had become a valued member of his ashram had a sad personal story and, as over four years had passed since he joined them, he might be able to talk about it.

'I left her, and came here to find you. After Jallianwala Bhag, I desired peace.'

'I suspected Jallianwala was the culprit.' Gandhi's eyes twinkled behind his round spectacles, 'The children of the ashram joked with me when I returned from the Punjab, saying, 'Look, Bapuji you went to the Punjab and sent us a Sikh. Do you remember?' They laughed together at the shared memory.

After a pause, 'Those who died in the Bhag are indeed martyrs, Basant. Because of them our struggle for self-rule has progressed. You have also been a great help in the ashram, but won't your wife be waiting for you?' Gandhi was always keen to help his disciples. Basant was estranged from his wife, and in Gandhi's view, should be reconciled.

'I have been thinking about that recently,' said Basant.

'I know a little bit about Sikhism. Isn't it true that Guru Nanak teaches his disciples not to forget the family: the best Sikh is the house-holder, isn't that the way? Ba and I also had problems, but we worked them out and now, as you see, we are very happy.'

'Yes, you are both quite content,' agreed Basant.

'The worst time was in South Africa when I insisted that everyone share the work: she couldn't find it in herself to clean the latrines, and she hated me then. It was against all her previous experience and values.'

'I found that very hard too,' Basant smiled.

Again there was a twinkle in Gandhi's eyes.

'Cleaning latrines teaches us so much, not just about ourselves but our attitude to others, and when we clean up after others, their attitude to us also changes.'

Basant nodded in agreement, however Ba came into the kitchen just then and the conversation ended.

A few weeks later Basant left the Sabarmati ashram, a changed man from the one who had arrived there. He was sad to leave, but he knew that he must return to his family commitments. He

186

could see that from within this ashram, Gandhi, living a simple life, was forging a change in India that would lead to freedom. His own contribution was best made from his work in Delhi and his life with his family in the Punjab.

Tirath was still employed at the construction company and lived in the same lodgings. Basant found his old job was available and returned to work.

'It's good to have you back,' said Tirath, 'Obviously you are feeling better, and you look refreshed.'

'I feel calmer. At the ashram, Bapuji encourages everyone to live simply and to share everything, including all the work, even the cleaning of the latrines – which we leave to untouchables. I've cleaned up a baby, but to face a latrine full of adult excrement is nothing like that. At first I was always retching, and even vomited from the smell.'

'When my father was ill and bed-ridden, I had to clean him, but he was family, and that's different,' agreed Tirath.

'As for spinning, in the Punjab it is seen as women's work, but Bapuji says it is good training for everyone. He spins for at least a half-hour each day, even in prison.'

'You call him father now,' smiled Tirath.

'We all did at the ashram. He could see that I had improved. For the first two years, I didn't speak at all: they accepted me without comment.'

'And when you did speak, how did you communicate with him? He is Gujarati and speaks neither Punjabi nor Hindi. Although I hear he is learning Hindi.'

'People who care for each other don't need language. Observation, simple gestures and facial expressions suffice, as they do for children.' They both laughed in agreement.

187

'Speaking of caring, there are letters here for you.' Tirath handed Basant a bundle of about thirty letters.

The first was from Takri, full of news about the extended family and the neighbours. Receiving no reply, in her next letter, she asked about his health and the news from Delhi. Then there was a letter from his aunt, about the baby's death and Takri's fragile state of mind and health, before and after the birth.

In the next letter from Takri, written by his cousin's son Surain, she said that she knew he was not working in Delhi, that she would manage to live on the money he'd left and would sew when her health improved. She would continue to write to him at the Delhi address in the hope that he would return there. The letter after that one was written in a badly-formed childish hand, with very poor spelling and no vowel indicators. Basant smiled, as he realised that Takri had started to learn to write Punjabi. She wrote how, after the baby's death, she could not have survived without the support of the women in the lane, especially Jenna. Had he heard that after Jallianwala the people had been made to crawl along the street in Amritsar, and been whipped by the soldiers as they crawled? Gandhi had visited the Punjab, welcomed by crowds of thousands in Lahore, and he'd called for self-rule for India. She had decided to follow him, burnt her two suits of mill-cloth and now would spin all that she required for her clothes and bedding.

Basant felt proud of her. Why had he imagined that the village would stand still? Bapuji's plan, to bring the villagers into politics, with everyone making a small contribution, was obviously working. He felt optimistic for the future and wrote home.

When the postman delivered his letter, Takri called for Surain. When he said it was from Delhi, in Chacha's own hand, she burst into tears at her spinning wheel.

Jenna was with them in the courtyard, rolling cotton for spinning. She cried, 'Praise be to Allah!'

'Do you want to read it yourself, Chachi? You can ask me if you can't read any of the words.'

'You've been a good teacher. I'll try,' sobbed Takri, wiping her tears.

'While you're reading, I'll put some water on for tea,' said Surain. Jenna agreed that was a good idea. Takri read slowly, and Surain was pleased when she didn't ask for any help.

'It's good news. He is working in Delhi again. Surain, could you read it out loud now?' asked Takri.

Three of the neighbouring women, including Durgee with a baby on her hip, joined them on seeing the postman stop at Takri's door, so Surain had an audience: he read in a clear voice.

Afterwards Takri said, 'There were times when I thought he would never come back.'

'I never doubted, because the holy man foretold it. You both suffered so much but it's over now, five years are long enough,' Jenna said. Everyone agreed.

Basant returned on a short leave during which he and Takri spent hours talking about the changes in their lives. They decided to try for a family again, and before Basant left he agreed that their next baby should be fostered, as the pir had advised. Takri became pregnant and made preparations for the baby's care after the birth.

'Will you manage to look after my baby for five years, Jenna?' Takri asked. 'Having a small baby will be a change for you.'

'Of course, I'll be delighted to do it. My boys are older and I'm not going to have any more children,' Jenna smiled. 'I will enjoy having a baby around the house again: we all will.'

A daughter was born to Takri. After forty days, she was weaned to goat's milk: Takri bought Jenna a cow so that she, Ali and the boys could have their own source of milk as thanks for their help. Jenna's family were very happy to have the baby live with them. They called her Saira, and spoiled her from the moment they woke up in the morning until they went to bed. When she was asleep they tip-toed about being careful not to wake her though Jenna insisted the baby was used to their noise.

Takri watched and prayed: the boys brought the baby up every evening so she could see her. Saira thrived. Jenna worked at the bazaar, frying popcorn, for two hours in the late afternoon. Baby Saira accompanied her foster-mother. The village knew that this baby was thriving due to the love between a Muslim and a Sikh family. Saira's name for Jenna was Ami as she heard her adoptive brothers call their mother. She called Takri by the title all the children in the lane used, Chachi, the younger aunt.

Two years later, when Takri gave birth to a boy she was reassured by Durgee. 'Don't worry, he'll be fine. Your daughter Saira has broken the bad luck spell. See how she happy she is with Jenna.'

But everyone watched over him with extra care. He was called Nirmal, and was followed two years later by another boy who was named Ajit. Takri's family was complete.

Early in 1930, Takri made preparations to join Basant in Delhi with the three children. Of course Jenna had known that she must return Saira when she was five, but she had mixed feelings about it. She was happy for Takri, grateful that the child had indeed thrived, but would miss the 'baby' of her family.

'We'll be back each summer, Jenna. Then you'll be reunited with Saira.'

'Yes, and don't forget I'm her Ami, her mother? You're only her Chachi, her aunt.' They laughed together.

CHAPTER TWO

Towards Independence 1930-1944

During the next six years as Basant and Takri raised their family in Delhi, the struggle for Independence continued. Although Basant had made his peace with what happened in Amritsar, in his heart he wished to see Karam again; to let him know the jealousy, that had clouded his brain in their last days together, had gone, and he still valued their friendship.

When Mahatma Gandhi walked to the sea to protest against the Salt Laws, Basant and Takri went to the ashram to walk part of the way with him.

'You lived here for nearly four years? It's very peaceful. How far is it from here to the sea?' Takri asked as she sat on the bank of the river Sabarmati with her feet in the water.

'It's about two hundred and fifty miles. The walk will take three weeks to a month,' replied Basant.

'Why is he walking and not taking the train? He doesn't look strong.'

'He's tougher than he looks. The media will report over a longer period of time than if it was a train journey, and Gandhi will gather support on the route. We'll see him off at the start and join him again near the sea.'

'He's an inspiration, highly educated but so humble. I feel privileged to have met him,' said Takri. 'But he'll never be alone on the walk?'

'Oh no, there's a chosen group of about seventy who will always be with him. He'll never be alone. They seem to be gathering for the send-off over there. Hear the cheers? Let's join them.'

Basant and Takri walked five miles to support the protest that first day, and then took the train back to Delhi and their young family. Three weeks later they travelled to Dandi, where the Mahatma was expected to lift salt from the seashore and break the law. When the group arrived at the beach, the world's press and hundreds of well-wishers were already there. Basant and Takri had taken up a position on rocks from where they could see the main group of satyagrahis, peaceful protestors. Gandhi made a speech calling for the British to repeal the law that taxed salt, making it an offence to gather this basic mineral from an Indian beach. Takri watched him bend down and lift a grain of salt from the beach and raise it into the air. If thunder and lightning had been heard at that moment she wouldn't have been surprised.

'And now he's heading for prison,' whispered Basant. 'The British can't ignore this.'

Takri heard a female voice shout, 'Hail! Deliverer!' and an almighty cheer went up from the crowd. Cameras clicked. Takri remembered the prison in Calcutta and wondered where Karam was: she looked around but he was not in the crowd.

As people gathered around the Mahatma, Basant took his wife's hand and led her towards the sea. They each lifted a grain of salt.

A young man walked past them saying, 'Let them arrest all of us. Do you know the British axed this tax in their own country nearly a hundred years ago and they're still taking money from us?'

'Yes, I know,' answered Basant, 'perhaps not for long now.'

He stood with Takri, looking out at the constantly rolling waves.

'What a wonderful sight,' she murmured, 'the sea meeting the sky.' They walked up and down the beach until evening, only returning to catch the train to Delhi when all was quiet except for the swish of the water.

'Chacha, take me with you,' Saira called as she ran to the gate of the courtyard. 'I've finished my sewing. Haven't I Chachi?'

'Yes, you've been working hard all morning,' Takri was laying out material for a new kameez for a neighbour who was sitting opposite her waiting to be measured.

'Come along then, we'll go together. Nehru's speaking today.'

Basant wheeled his bicycle through the gate and waited as Saira seated herself on the shelf behind him.

At the rallies, Basant always looked around for Karam. He had even gone to the local Congress Party group, asking about him. They told him many of the Sikhs, including Karam had left the party to follow the militants and they'd lost touch with him.

Otherwise, life was good for the family. Saira and the boys were bright and attended school. She learned Punjabi whilst they studied the official language, Urdu. After school the boys took part in sports, and Saira learned home-making skills with her mother. Takri was happy, and amongst the Sikh community in Delhi she had many friends.

Basant was happy in his work but one morning as he climbed on scaffolding to measure up for a window frame, the bamboo struts collapsed under his weight.

As the dust settled, men came forward. 'It's Basant. Don't move him. Call for a doctor.'

'He's unconscious. We must take him to hospital,' was the doctor's advice, 'I'll tell his family on my way home.'

Takri spent the night by Basant's bedside. In the morning the doctor said, 'his sight may improve but I am not hopeful.'

Two months later, Basant gave up his job and was offered a monthly pension or a one-off payment. Basant accepted the lump sum, which he saved for Saira's wedding.

The family returned to Rurka to straitened circumstances. The neighbours gathered to commiserate with the family. The village saint, Chinta, came to sit with Basant and wept to see him helpless and blind. The children's schooling ceased, but fortunately the boys were given work as young apprentices in a local workshop. Nirmal was eleven and Ajit eight; and they were paid one rupee a month. Saira had learned to sew clothes, knit sweaters and to spin and weave, and helped her mother to make a little money using these skills. They lived on whatever they earned each day. When they couldn't afford vegetables, there was always pickle to eat with chapattis.

At first the boys had been cleaning around the workshop and running errands, but as they grew older they learned to turn lathes, producing nuts and bolts. World War Two was a boom time for the small workshops in the Punjab. It was through work that they met Jai who had been sent from Goraya to help set up and operate a new machine. He was only three years older than Nirmal, but at seventeen he had worked in the bigger towns and learned new techniques on the lathe. The boys came home and mentioned that they had made a new friend at the workshop.

'He is called Jai and comes from Goraya,' said Ajit.

Basant said, 'Ask him his father's name. Perhaps I know him.'

When Nirmal came home and said, 'Bhagwan Singh is his father,' Takri smiled and told them of the day she and Basant had gone to a house in Goraya near the Grand Gate, and 'looked at' a boy who might be a suitable match for Saira. He was the one and a betrothal took place, as Takri sat him on her knee to receive the gifts of a dried date and one rupee from her.

'He is your brother-in-law to be,' Takri told her boys. 'I hope you were polite to him.'

'Yes,' both nodded excited and a bit awed by the news.

'The year after next we will have a wedding for Saira and Jai. You must call him Bhaiyaji. He's like an elder brother,' Takri advised.

'What else do you know about him?' asked Ajit.

'We know that Jai's family have lived in Goraya for twelve generations. It's destined to become a big town because of its position on the Great Trunk Road and the railway.'

'Everybody knows that,' said Ajit, raising his eyes, 'But do you know anything else about Jai? I mean Bhaiya.'

Takri added, 'They have a saint in the family. Rishi, Jai's great-grandfather's brother, who became a Hindu holy man. He gave his land to a group of monks who made it their ashram. You've been there, the temple on the GT Road.'

'We went last Baisakhi. Hey, Saira, you're going to be married into the family of a famous holy man, isn't that

196

impressive?' asked Nirmal smiling across at Saira who bent her head over her sewing, like a dutiful daughter, pretending not to listen.

Basant ignored Nirmal, and continued, 'Jai's grandfather was quite a village entrepreneur, a good example for you boys. He managed a team of men who went out to the villages around Goraya to help when the crops were gathered, or the fields ploughed. Later, he built bullock carts, and when these became less common, he fitted tyres to carts and motorised vehicles. And then, in his later years I'm told he bought two water buffalo, to sell milk. He built a house near the Grand Gate.'

'Is that the house Saira will live in?'

'Yes, it's the house where Jai was born. His father has made trips to Kenya to work, and earned enough money to rebuild the house. It's built of red brick and quite spacious, much bigger than ours.'

'Isn't Saira lucky to have in-laws like that? When's the wedding?' asked Nirmal.

'You must ask your mother,' said Basant.

'It has to be November because that's Lord Krishna's month, and not for another two years when Saira will be eighteen,' Takri stated.

She sighed at the memory of how Easrie's in-laws had asked for her to live with them soon after the wedding: now most girls were married when they were older and had been to school. They left to live with their husbands the day after the wedding. Just as she had always felt it was right to do.

'Your mother is a believer in Hindu customs, but it will do no harm to appease her, November it will be,' Basant whispered to Ajit, as his son guided him to bed. Basant's blindness meant he only required help in places new to him.

Although he was good around the house without his stick, the boys always wanted to help. He made his own way to the bazaar, and that was where he spent his time, listening to news, and chatting with anyone who stopped to sit beside him.

The brothers were excited about having Jai at the workshop, but he was going to be there for only a few more days, so they introduced themselves.

'I know,' he answered with a laugh. 'My mother told me last night when I said I had been to Rurka to work. I was betrothed when I was little, and needed a reminder.'

'Tell us about your family,' asked Ajit who wanted to know everything about his future brother-in-law.

'Well, the most famous person in my family, as you probably know, is Baba Rishi. I would have called him Baba because of his relationship to me, but now he is everyone's grandfather.'

'Yes, he is a revered holy man who belongs to everyone. I think it's good that we have a link with him, through you, Bhaiya. And your grandfather, he was rich.'

'Hmm. Well, my grandfather was wealthy and very secretive. The house we live in now used to be the family house. When my grandparents left, it was a surprise to everyone that he'd bought another house. But if you asked him he'd say my grandmother was the head of the house. I remember him well, a big, cheerful man.'

All too soon, lunchtime was over, and the boys went back to work.

In the evening Ajit related the conversation to Basant and Takri.

'I like him,' grinned Ajit, 'he works really fast on the machine. Did you know that he left school after three years? Just like me. And he learned to turn the lathe at his brother-in-law's workshop in Phagwara. As for carpentry, he learned it from his father and grandfather.'

'Go to sleep boys. It's late,' scolded Basant, 'you are obviously so pleased with your brother-in-law that you could talk about him all night.'

'Ye-es Chacha,' Nirmal and Ajit chimed in unison and climbed the stairs to the rooftop.

In the morning when they had both gone to work, as Takri and Saira were preparing for the day's sewing, Basant said, 'I wonder what stories they will come back with tonight. This is an exciting time for them.'

'Yes,' replied Takri, 'You'd think that they themselves had found Jai for Saira. But it's good to see them happy.'

At the workshop, during a break for tea, Ajit said to Jai, 'Tell us more about your family, Bhaiya.'

'I'll tell you a story,' Jai began, smiling mischievously, 'which I've always thought amusing. It's about my grandmother's habit of burying money. My grandfather worked hard and could have bought property as an investment, but my grandmother only felt safe if she buried their money. We all lived together in the family house, but one day my grandparents left, without explanation, taking everything. My youngest uncle was unmarried and still lived with them so he helped to pack the brass dishes, the low wooden stools, the almirahs and beds that they owned. They also dug up the brass money jar from the store room. They didn't believe that my parents really had no money. But we didn't and my mother was very upset until my father suggested looking in the store room for anything that might have been left. At the spot where the brass jar had been dug up they found a ten Malika coin in the earth.'

199

'A Malika coin? I've not heard of it.' asked Ajit.

'It's a lot of money.'

'Yes, the Malika is the Empress Victoria. That one coin helped my parents after my grandparents' departure. My father had always helped them financially since he'd begun work as a boy, so he kept it.'

'That was lucky when they had no money. Has your father always worked in Goraya?' asked Nirmal.

'No. He went to Kenya in Africa to work for about five years. That helped him with the weddings of my two sisters and my brother. So things are easier now.'

'We hope to start a workshop of our own. We have learned how to run the business,' whispered Nirmal.

'Yes, I'll handle the workshop, and Nirmal will look for customers for us. That's our plan,' joined in Ajit.

'Sounds good. I may go to Ludhiana soon. It's a growing city with plenty of work.'

Later in the day, the foreman of the workshop said to Jai, 'I hear this is your last day with us. We've learned a lot from you.'

'I have enjoyed being here.' Jai said goodbye to the boys, and walked the six miles home to Goraya. At the gatehouse, the Grand Gate, he greeted the community elders who sat under the ancient banyan tree. Waving to the children playing under the veranda he stopped at a fire where a woman who sat frying popcorn gave him a handful as he passed.

'Thanks, Chachi,' he smiled.

Once home, he shouted, 'I'm back,' to let his mother know.

Jai could hear the slip-slap of her chapattis as she cooked them on her griddle, and busied himself having a bucket bath, changing into clean clothes and joining his father for their evening meal. Jai's mother was a tall, elegant woman who was looking forward to her younger son's wedding to see him settled. She had no gold to give his bride, but she knew his in-laws were not wealthy so they wouldn't expect much. All of her four children would be married within a five-mile radius of Goraya which was good as her own parents were about fifty miles away to the east and she could only visit once every few years.

CHAPTER THREE

Partition 1947

Takri wanted a simple wedding for Saira, she was afraid there was a curse on the girls of the family, because Bhani and Easrie had been widowed young.

'We don't want to attract the evil eye, through any lavish celebrations,' said Takri, 'I was unhappy for so long, Jenna. You'll remember.'

'Yes, but that's in the past, Takri. People are healthier, and villages cleaner now.'

Takri and Basant went to Mehatpur to give invitations. While Basant stayed with Dara, who was now in his eighties, Takri visited neighbours to tell them her good news. One of these was Karam's mother.

'Is it Takri? Come sit near me daughter, I'm almost blind now. Let me touch your face. You haven't come to Mehatpur since your grandmother died?'

'That's right, Auntie. I have been busy with my children.'

'It's through our children growing up that we know time passes. I'm old now, and I so miss not seeing my Karam. He was a few years older than you. Do you remember him?'

'Yes, I do.' Takri felt as if everything had stopped for a second. A vision of the scene at Jallianwala Bhag came before her eyes, with Karam, carrying her son's body, shouting for her to

202

follow him out, and then with a gasp, she brought herself back to the present.

'Are you alright, my dear? Drink some water,' the old lady continued, 'I think he was never the same after Jallianwala. That was when I last saw him. One sand-stormy night he came in, wild-eyed and desperate, I thought he'd gone mad. All night he tossed and turned. He drank the tea I brewed for him and before dawn he was gone. For years afterwards I would wake early, brew tea and walk the path I thought he had taken, hoping perhaps he'd return that way, but he didn't. Oh ...,' with a deep sigh, 'enough of the past, tell me about your daughter.'

'My Saira is more like her father. She has a touch of falveri, patches of white skin while his skin is all white. You remember, Auntie? He is albino.'

'Yes. The whole village was shocked at your father's decision for you to marry an albino. But you've been alright, haven't you dear?'

'I've made the best of it, Auntie. We all make compromises,' admitted Takri. 'I told Saira's mother-in-law about her colouring: she said as long as she has both eyes and isn't a cripple her skin colour does not matter.'

'A wise woman,' responded Karam's mother, 'We villagers have enough problems without bringing skin colour into them. Ah, here's some tea. Takri, have you met my grandson's wife?'

Takri left as soon as she could. She had fulfilled her duty by visiting Karam's mother, but talking about him was difficult. She wondered where he was, for in her heart she knew he was alive, his mother did too. He had covered his tracks well, but was living somewhere, hiding the pain, as she was. Sometimes she thought of the pir who had foretold that the man she loved

203

would return. At the time, the thought had occurred to her, does he see Basant or Karam? And if he did return, how would she look him in the face, knowing that she had given away their daughter, perhaps his only child, to a brothel? This was the reason she seldom came to Mehatpur. It brought back memories best buried in her heart. She had an understanding with Basant and she didn't want it disturbed.

Takri's sisters attended Saira's wedding. Jenna helped in the organisation, with her sons acting as Saira's elder brothers. The wedding party arrived in horse-carriages, staying two nights to enable the rituals and traditions to be observed with dignity, and then they left for Goraya with the bride. Jenna's son took her in his carriage, weeping as he left: his baby sister was grown up and gone to a new home. He was comforted by neighbours and wedding guests.

Eighteen months later, Saira returned to her parents' home for her first confinement, and her son Jaspal was born during the monsoon. Sitting in a shop in the bazaar, with the warm rain falling, water overflowing the gutters and flooding the street, Basant heard that the dropping of the atomic bomb on Japan had ended the Second World War. As families in the Punjab waited for soldiers to come home, the Congress Party knew Independence was close but the price was a division that would enable Muslims to live, as a majority, in the new country of Pakistan.

'The Congress doesn't want it, but the Muslim League is pressing for a separate country.' The young shopkeeper read the article to Basant.

'Will the Punjab be divided? This is where there are most Muslims,' asked Basant.

'The border will certainly split the state, but we don't know where. We must prepare to move at short notice.'

'I can't leave Rurka, son,' said Basant.

'It will be the law. We may have no choice, Chacha.'

Muslims, Hindus and Sikhs in Rurka waited for the new border to be announced. At first, it was rumoured to be set at Jullundur, twenty-two miles from Goraya. Takri kept a bundle of clothes and provisions ready to take, afraid that the call to move from their homes might come in the middle of the night. When the border was announced, it was between Lahore and Amritsar, and the Muslim families in Rurka knew it was they who must leave to start a new life in Pakistan. Knowing that they would now be separated, Jenna told Takri about her daughter, the baby given to the courtesan.

They stood together in the back room whispering, 'I cannot keep this to myself, because who knows what the future holds, Takri? We didn't think our world would change like this. I must tell you about your child.'

'I may never be able to look for her. How do you know she is alive? Have you seen her?'

'When you were living in Delhi the troupe made a tour of this area. She was fourteen, healthy and beautiful. My aunt, who had taken the place of the madam and had power, had brought her to keep her safe and let her work as a maid. She told me she hadn't allowed her to become a child prostitute; she was at school, quick at learning, and extremely talented in music. It was the last time that I saw them. You must memorise this address, we can't write it down.'

'Yes, tell me' answered Takri.

'Nur is the adopted child of Sajida Begum who lives at House Number 1, Babur Chowk, The Friday Mosque Road, Old Delhi.'

'Yes,' Takri sighed, 'My dear daughter. Nur. House Number One. Babur Chowk. Old Delhi.'

'They may not go to Pakistan. I hear some people in the cities are choosing to remain in India.'

'God bless you, Jenna.'

'May Allah be with you, my dear, and with His grace we will meet again.'

There was no pressure on the Muslims in Rurka to move, as had happened in other villages, but finally they were escorted to a refugee holding camp in Ludhiana. Believing that once people settled down in Pakistan they would be free to return, they left their homes with promises of meeting again, giving assurances of writing letters on arrival. Saira, came, through the monsoon rain, from Goraya to pay a last visit. Jenna's house already looked abandoned; she was frying closed corn kernels, which were easy to carry. They embraced, in tears vowed to write, and visit when they could in a peaceful future.

Later, Saira heard that they were still in the camp, awaiting military escort over the border. There was news of atrocities on both sides. In Goraya a call went out for volunteers to lay siege to the nearby walled town of Talwan where the Muslim population had refused to leave.

The call went up, 'They've burned the gurdwara!'

'We don't want them here. Let's get rid of the sons of pigs. If they won't go, they'll die.'

The vigilantes surrounded the town, where the Muslims had closed the gates, after Hindu and Sikh families had fled. The siege lasted three days, until those outside were given information that the Muslims in the town were not as heavily armed as they had thought: then they scaled the walls. No-one was spared, young men caught up in the horror, returned to their homes with blood on their swords and grim, closed faces, unwilling to divulge the truth of the attack on Talwan and its aftermath.

Saira was left with no news of Jenna and her family. Ultimately, she had to accept that the lack of contact from them meant they were amongst the thousands who had died at the birth of Pakistan. Takri sat on the perimeter wall of Jenna's rooftop and grieved for her friend.

CHAPTER FOUR

Jai 1947-1953

Following Partition, there was a shortage of employment, Jai moved to the larger towns along the G.T. Road nearer Delhi: he was away from home for long periods.

When he was back in Goraya, for a short time at the end of 1948, a skilled twenty-three year old with a wife and two children, his work was noticed by a friend who had recently returned from Britain.

'You should go to England. They're advertising for workers from India.'

'I have a lot of experience in carpentry and on the lathe. I would like to go abroad,' Jai answered.

His father interrupted, 'I spent years in Africa. To go abroad isn't always the best option.'

'I've worked in all the towns between here and Delhi, why not in England?' argued Jai.

'Well,' the friend continued, 'if you do decide to go, there is an agent in Goraya who is preparing documents for some other men. I'll introduce you to him.'

Jai knew his parents would be unhappy at his leaving because the money he earned was a useful addition to their household income. He thought this was a chance to get away and be free to use his earnings the way he wanted, although he would always send them money. The amount required for the passport and flight to London was two thousand rupees, part of which Jai secured as a loan from his sister's husband, whilst his father funded the rest. In four days his passport and travel documents were ready. Saira was told of his departure the night before he was due to leave. She sat veiled, cradling her almost one-year old daughter, under the oil lamp.

Jai's father said to her, 'Jai's going tomorrow, and it is very far away: further than East Africa. We'll not see him for a long time. Have you anything to say about it?'

She did not answer as she was used to being told only what was deemed necessary by the family, but this came as a shock. He always came home every few months but this would mean separation for years.

'She cannot have any say in this,' Jai cut in, he did not want her to make a negative comment, 'we need money to live. Who's going to earn it? Not her father, that's for sure.'

Saira winced at the insult to her blind father, and her own poverty, replying with the expected answer from a powerless wife, 'It is for the best. I have no objection.'

That December day in Goraya, Jai left the house to wait at the railway station for the train to Delhi, which was delayed for twelve hours, but he wouldn't go back to the house. He spent most of the night on the platform, with his mother's words ringing in his ears. She was obviously sad at his going, but he knew the knowledge that her elder son had left and not supported them financially, worried her. She thought he would do the same.

'Since you're so keen to leave, don't come back until I send for you.' She had spoken sharply to him.

'I'll remember you said that to me. I'll not return until you write and ask me,' was his reply.

Waiting for the train, he thought it was poverty that made them cruel to each other. When he came back he would not be poor, he'd have his own car, a German car. It was a cold winter's night, one he would remember all of his days, full of bitter partings and unsaid goodbyes, yet with hope for a better future. Before the train arrived a fellow traveller asked him where he was going.

'To England,' Jai replied.

'My brother has been over there for a few years. I'll give you his address, you never know, it might come in useful.'

Jai watched while the stranger wrote on a page of a small notebook, tearing the paper out to hand to him.

'Gurdev Singh is my brother. He lives in a city called Glasgow. Good Luck.'

The stranger boarded a local train leaving Jai wondering what the future held. He felt as if he'd left Goraya and his old life behind, although he was still sitting on the station platform.

In Delhi two other men were met at the station, by the agent, and the group spent the night at his home.

'I will accompany you to the airport tomorrow to iron out any problems. Your papers are completely in order, but you can't trust these officials,' he explained, 'You can relax until morning. I have the Holy Book upstairs, so you may wish to pay your respects.'

In the morning at Pallam International Airport the officials checked the passports of the three men, asking unnecessary and irritating questions.

'Who is this young man?'

'This is Jai Singh, my own son,' the agent lied. 'What is the problem?'

Later, when he said goodbye to them he was still grumbling about the attitude of the officials, 'They are suspicious of everyone, especially Sikhs wearing turbans.'

The passports and tickets passed the next inspection, and the three men boarded the flight. The plane stopped at Beirut, Frankfurt, Amsterdam and finally London. In all, the journey took two days.

Near Heathrow Airport, most Sikh immigrants stopped off in the town of Southall, before moving on to other locations. Many settled there, earning the name Little India for the London suburb. In Jai's case he grew restless after a few weeks of unemployment. Hearing about the industrial towns in the north, he showed a friend the address that the stranger at Goraya station had given him.

'That's in Scotland. There's a lot of shipbuilding and other industry there, probably more your line of work.'

Jai left Euston Station, arriving at Glasgow Central on a grey, foggy evening. He showed the elderly taxi driver the paper with Gurdev Singh's address.

'Aye. Get ye'er sel' in lad. It's doon the road.' Realising the young man in the turban, carrying the one small suitcase, couldn't understand him, the taxi driver gestured to his vehicle, waving him on to the seat. He drove along Argyle Street for only two hundred yards, before reaching Anderston Cross. Taking the money, he walked in front of him, up the stairs of the close to the first floor. It was where he knew a group of this lad's kin lived, he could tell from their cloth hats.

He beat loudly on the door and shouted, 'Yer boy's here.' As the door opened, he winked at Jai, and took his leave saying, 'Ther' ye' are, laddie. They'll look after ye.'

Gurdev said, 'Sat siri akal,' to the young man at the door, who stepped forward to shake his hand, replying with the same words. He opened the door wider and ushered him in. Eight men shared the flat. Four were on shifts, so the beds were used day and night. Jai went in search of a job round the industrial factories that might require his skills. Meanwhile he saw other men working as pedlars, and thought it was a good second job to do in his spare time. People here stopped work at five, and Saturday and Sunday seemed to be holidays. In India he'd worked every day.

'It's easy to be a pedlar,' Gurdev explained, 'you buy the clothes at the warehouse and take them from door to door. We'll tell you where to go, so you're not encroaching on someone else's route: it's only a problem if a Muslim brother, or a Bhatra Sikh, already works the area. The people know that you're selling something, you show them your licence at the door, and they'll want to see the clothes in your suitcase. Then they'll tell you what they really want, and you go back with their stuff the following week - you'll have customers!'

'I could do this in the evenings, once I've got a day job, and at the weekends. I want to work all the time. My family back home need the money.'

'That's what we're all here for, and when we've got enough money we can all go home. It's mostly the white women who want the clothes, and a good-looking chap like you shouldn't have any trouble at all,' smiled Gurdev, mischieviously, 'Oh and get your hair cut before a girl opens the door to her house, and faints at your feet. Isn't that right Sucha?'

'Absolutely.' Sucha, who was shaving at the kitchen sink, joined in the laughter. 'After the girl fainted at the sight of my turban and beard, I got the hair off, pretty damn quick.'

212

'Did you go back to her house?' asked Jai.

'Yes. They didn't recognise me without my beard: they're good customers now. I apologise every time I see the girl.'

Jai applied for a pedlar's licence from the police office. He packed a suitcase at the warehouse, where the Punjabi-speaking Muslim owner gave him credit, and helped him choose the most popular items. Taking his flatmates' advice, he paid a visit to the barber who cut his long hair, and shaved his beard. He bought a trilby hat and a long light-brown woollen coat to complete his new look. His lack of language was a slight problem, but the peddling became easier with time. If he knocked on a door, and the person opening it swore and slammed it shut, he moved to the next house. He learned to recognise the swear words, but refused to be aroused to anger. If the householder took a minute to look at him and his licence, then he would be invited in, and this gave him a chance to see how the Scottish people lived. He was an attractive young man, medium height, light-skinned, slim and with a pleasant manner. Women liked him, and he enjoyed watching them look through the contents of his suitcase. They realised his English was poor, and took time to explain, even writing down their requirements. Gurdev had taught him to say, 'I come back in one week.' Later, when his main job required him to work night shift, he told his regular customers he would return in two weeks. If they wanted to pay in instalments he kept a book, and collected the money from them on each visit. It was easy work, and good money, compared to what he'd done in India.

At the warehouse, while choosing clothes for his customers, he started chatting to a tall, slim man who could have been any religion but for the kara which slid down his jacket sleeve. He held a lady's cardigan up to the light.

'I have a customer who wants a cardigan like that one, but not that colour. Have you seen in it green?' He asked in Punjabi knowing the man would understand him and curious that he hadn't met him before. When the man turned to look at him he added, 'Sat siri akal ji,' and stretched out his hand.

'Sat siri akal, son.' A strong grip held Jai's hand: a steady green-brown gaze met his. 'This is the colour the lady I'm buying for will like. I haven't seen it green. You're new in Glasgow?'

'Yes, sir. Jai Singh from Goraya.'

'Kamaljit Singh from Jalandhar,, but I left thirty years ago. Hardly anyone will remember me. Goraya, eh?'

'We're almost neighbours back home then. I'm staying at Gurdev's.'

'I should come round, haven't seen Gurdev for a while. Look forward to seeing you again, Jai Singh.'

Later Jai told Gurdev he'd met Kamaljit Singh.

'Yes, I know him. Keeps his own company a lot. We think he was a fugitive from the Raj. One of Bhagat Singh's group of saboteurs. He's well settled here with a Scottish wife.'

Through the migrant's grapevine Jai was told of a factory where lathe turners were required, so he went along to the factory in Queenslie Industrial Estate, looking for a job. The foreman who met him brought along a Pakistani worker, as an interpreter.

'Are you carpenter/ironworker caste?' he asked Jai in Punjabi.

'Yes, I am.'

Turning to the foreman the worker said, 'This chap is from the caste of machine workers in India. They're born engineers, and start working young. If he seems confident he's probably very good.'

The foreman took Jai to the lathe, giving him a chance to show his skills at producing nuts and bolts to specific measurements. Jai was fast and accurate for he'd been working on similar machines since he was a boy. The foreman was pleased to take him on.

When he had a little spare cash, he posed for a portrait in his new western style of dress, new suit and trilby hat, and sent a copy to Goraya. When Jai's photo arrived his parents were not surprised or unhappy about him discarding his Sikh turban and beard; they'd been through this with their elder son, who while living in Lahore had shed his turban ten years before. Jaspal saw the photo at the farm, and ran to the house at the Grand Gate to tell his mother.

'Papaji has sent a photo. I saw it, his hair is cut,' he told Saira excitedly.

The photo remained at the farm, until Saira asked to see it. Then Jaspal was allowed to bring it to the house.

He said, 'Look, Rupa. It's Papaji.'

Saira smiled.

CHAPTER FIVE

Glasgow 1954 - 1955

Jai bought a flat for his family when they joined him in Scotland. He was earning a good wage, making profits from his peddling business as well as from letting out rooms to lodgers.

His Sikh friends insisted, 'We will all return to the Punjab so why send for our families?'

Undaunted he sent sponsorship papers to Saira at her father's address.

Saira, eight year old Jaspal, and five year old Rupa, flew to join Jai in Glasgow arriving at London's Heathrow Airport on a bleak February evening. Rupa hid behind her mother as she did not know this man in the trilby hat and long coat: all the men in her family wore turbans and beards. Saira looked at him shyly, although absolutely delighted to see him. Their behaviour would always be as it was when they were first married: all show of marital affection was kept for the night.

Their second son Ranjit was born in the high-ceilinged large front room of their flat, after a long labour. Following the traditional forty days, Saira made ludoos to distribute amongst their Punjabi friends, Sikh and Muslim to mark the baby's arrival.

It was a warm afternoon in June but Saira still wore her long, light brown wool coat with a bright headscarf knotted under her

216

chin. In the west of Scotland the weather could change from sunny in the morning to cold and wet by the afternoon. As it had on this day, the pavements were wet and people carried umbrellas ready for the next shower. She bustled out of the greengrocer's with her potatoes and carrots in a cotton bag, laying it in the basket under the baby's pram. Behind her a stout woman she met every day on her round of shopping manoeuvred herself to the side of the pram to gaze at Saira's baby son.

'Oh, he's grown since last week. They all look angelic when they're sleeping, don't they?'

Saira nodded and smiled although she didn't understand all the words. It was obvious the woman was chatting about the baby.

'See you again tomorrow, dear. Hope the weather lasts,' the woman smiled, waved her hand and walked towards the butcher's shop next door. Saira was grateful for the contact, thinking how friendly people were, though she felt inadequate when she couldn't speak to them.

As she pushed away from the door, an elderly man wearing a long, grey jacket and a trilby hat said, 'Sat Sri Akal' to her. She was startled but he had kind green-brown eyes and looked as if he knew her, but she was sure she hadn't met him before.

'Your bag looks quite heavy for the pram. Let me carry it for you. It's good to meet someone from the Punjab.'

'Sat siri akal ji. It's alright. I live quite near, over the hill.'

'I'd like to help. I'm from Jalandhar in the Punjab.'

'My home town is Rurka. We're in the same district, then,' Saira remarked, letting him carry the bag.

217

As they climbed the hill to Grafton Square they could hear the school bell ring, though it was in the other street and a row of tenements was between them. Then the shuffling, chatting, screaming and giggling sounds of the pupils carried on the breeze, and at the corner of the square two children came hurrying up behind them.

'This is Jaspal, my son, and that's Rupa. They will help me now. Thanks,' said Saira. She didn't tell the man her name, that didn't seem right, even in this country where everyone was so free.

As the boy reached for the bag Karam introduced himself as Kamaljit Singh.

Jaspal replied, 'Perhaps you know my father. His name is Jai Singh.'

'Yes, I know Jai. All the Sikhs in Glasgow know each other. You have your schoolbag to carry, Jaspal. I'll take this to your close. I'm going that way, and then I'll continue on down the hill to George Square.

'You know your way about Glasgow: you've been here a long time?' asked Saira.

'Yes, I've lived here since before the war.'

At the close the woman, who looked so like Takri, except for those white patches near her forehead and ears ... those reminded him of Basant's albinism, smiled at him, and said, 'sat siri akal' in farewell. He replied with the same words, shook the boy's hand, patted the little girl's head, and walked down the hill in a happy mood, thinking that if he couldn't live near Takri, it felt good to know he would not be far from her daughter. He'd put off this meeting: Jai had told him before his family had arrived, that his wife was from Rurka. He was afraid that a

218

familiar face from the past might cause upheaval in his peaceful life, but the meeting hadn't been so bad. He liked them and the past was not their fault. He would pay them a visit one evening.

It was now several months since his first visit and the old memories seemed to return to haunt him. Those longings for a certain woman's love and fears for his friendship with her husband. Should he return to India? He'd fought the British but they no longer ruled; he wasn't a fugitive from the law any more. Takri and Basant had continued with their lives, their marriage. Surely, his friend wouldn't blame him for one lapse. Time healed and he knew Basant was blind now. If he returned and found that Basant was still bitter about the past then he would leave the Punjab for good. Yes, that might work. Next year, perhaps?

He walked down John Street, from Jai's house, following another of his visits and was at the Cenotaph in a sunny and busy George Square before he realised he'd made the big decision. Tramcars trundled along the road, taking workers home, as Karam gazed at the massive stone lions sitting guard at the City Chambers. My war is over, he thought, it's time to return and make amends if that's what's necessary. I'll discuss my trip with Betty tonight. He joined the queue of people at the stop and boarded a tram for the west end.

When he alighted behind him was Kelvingrove Park, the trees covered in lush green leaves with only here and there a few yellow or orange ones heralding the autumn. He walked between the rows of dark grey tenements while the evening closed in, looking forward to Betty's smile and a hot dinner. He lifted his hat to a neighbour before entering the close and climbing the stairs to the second floor. Betty liked living here; she had friends nearby; though it was only a one-bedroom flat with cold running water. They used the public baths for a weekly swim and a hot bath to wash all over; another world from the running water of the well on his land in India, but he pushed that thought away.

'I'm home,' he called as he closed the door of the flat.

'Hello,' Betty came out of the kitchen for a kiss and then disappeared back to her cooking, as Karam hung up his coat and hat.

Later, after the meal of cold meat, potatoes and tinned peas, they sat sipping tea at the kitchen table. Both avoided each other's gaze until both spoke at once.

'You first,' smiled Karam.

'There was a letter from my cousin.'

'From Ireland?'

'My uncle is ill. Did I tell you, I used go there every year when I was a girl? If I let myself think about it, I realise how much I miss the countryside.'

'It's the same for me. If I let myself think about India ... Yes, the same. Do you want to visit?'

'It might be a long visit, that's the thing. What were you going to say?'

'Something similar. I wanted to talk to you about going to India.'

'Oh. So ... if I was in Ireland and you in India, at the same time, then neither of us would be left alone. That's quite convenient. Isn't it?'

'How do you feel about it? Being apart, I mean,' Karam gazed at her face, framed with white hair now, lines around her mouth and eyes which reminded him of the passing years. They hadn't married but it had never seemed important to either of them.

'Perhaps I could go to India another year and you could come to Ireland, the next time,' she said this almost gratefully. Karam sighed for he'd thought this would be a difficult conversation.

'That's settled then. After Christmas?' He took her cup and putting it into the sink, he gave it a wash. He added, 'Let's give this house up and find another place to live.'

'Somewhere with hot running water,' Betty smiled.

'Yes, Grafton Square seems nice, indoor bathrooms, stairways with windows and it's nearer the shops in town. You might like it more than here.'

'You mean rent one of Jai's flats?'

'We could ask him to look after our belongings and then move in when we return. That young man is no fool. He works, has a business selling clothes and is buying up the tenement block to let out,' Karam laughed. 'He's got four flats now.'

'They're certainly very careful with money,' Betty came up behind Karam as he stood at the sink looking at the lighted windows in the tenements across the road. She put her arms around him and laid her head on his shoulder.

'But, that's not all, Kam, is it?' You're in love with their little girl,' she tickled him, giggled and moved back quickly before he could turn and catch her.

'So are you, Betty Flynn, I've seen the way you look at her.' Karam had turned from the sink to sit down again and Betty did so too, careful to keep out of his reach.

'Why don't they pay more attention to her? The parents and her brother treat her like an outsider,' she said.

'If you think of how their investing in property, in the same way, they're putting time and effort into the boys. She'll be married off and spend her life with her in-laws. Jai didn't even tell me he had a daughter before their arrival. He talked about his wife and son. And Saira, she introduced her son but pointed and said, 'that's Rupa.' I was surprised even in that second the little girl stood to one side of them.'

'Yes, she's so grown up for her age and so excited about school.'

'She's not a child in the western sense at all. And now, school is her whole life. And the prize book ...,' Karam chuckled.

Betty interrupted, 'Oh the book it's all she has ... and her mother has commandeered it for her own use. Did you see, Kam? The airmail letters are in it and it's put high up. Oh, I so want to buy Rupa a doll? Will that be too much?' Betty's eyes filled.

'Will she know how to play with it? Ah, you see, you're in love with Rupa, Betty Flynn!'

'We're in the market for adopting a grandchild. So we must move to Grafton Square.'

'That would be good,' Karam gazed out of the window again, 'when we live near them, we'll give Rupa lots of attention.'

Betty added, 'Yes, when I'm back from Ireland and you've had your India trip. Visited all your old haunts, looked up your old flames. Those dusky Indian beauties,' her lilting, teasing laugh mingled with his deep hearty chuckle.

CHAPTER SIX

Delhi 1956

Jasmine had not lied, she was an expert; he paid her a generous tip for her services. She whispered that at one o'clock she would come out of the lane and walk in the direction of the Friday Mosque; all this she had been planning while he thought she was all his, what a master of her craft! She would wear her burkha, fully covered in black, but would be in a pink salwar that would show under the hem. The dhaba across the road served delicious meals. She would cross over to it and walk past him, he should follow.

Twenty minutes later he was walking out of the gate more sprightly than when he'd gone in. The gatekeeper gave him a deep bow.

Karam sat at the first table across the road from the entrance to the lane. The boy worker placed a tray with tea and biscuits in front of him. Later the proprietor brought over Karam's parathas and yoghurt.

'Please tell me it's none of my business, but you came out of the red lane this morning. I can't help but notice as I work across from it, day in day out.'

'Yes, I did. It is a place of many secrets,' Karam gave a little smile, 'and intrigues. I was disappointed. Have you always been at this dhaba?'

'My father owned it before me; I have worked here since I was eight.'

Karam thought he seemed a genuine fellow. There was no harm in asking. The man must be over fifty. 'Then do you remember the courtesan Sajida?'

'Ah, Sajida the beautiful, the enigmatic, fair as the moon; she who was always beyond my reach,' he stood to attention with his hand on his heart then raising his arm to the sky. 'How could anyone forget Sajida? You have returned from a foreign land ... England? Your clothes and manner give you away. Did you wish to find her here still?' He smiled and nodded in understanding.

'Yes, a simple desire, is it not?'

'And from your visit to the red lane, you know she has passed away.' He sat down at the next table, the one behind the kitchen, the big pot bubbling with the day's pulses, traditionally the black urid dahl.

Karam was wary of him. He could be in the pay of the madam.

The proprietor continued, 'what a grand funeral, it was. Everyone in the red lane turned out, there must be two thousand people working in that square over there. The men in front, the women, all in burkhas walking behind, weeping. We all wept.' He leaned his head on his hand. 'The whole street ceased business. When the bier passed, even the devotees came out of the mosque. All stopped in respect. When did you see her last, sir?'

'It must be almost thirty years. I came to watch her sing and dance before I left but on that day, I couldn't go in to the hall to watch for the crowds. I sat on the stairs, like many others, and listened from there.'

'You wouldn't know of her kindness when she became the madam. News like this wouldn't reach you in England. In this street we remember her as a friend. If we needed money when business was slow she was the first person we went to, and everyone has bad times: she always helped. But that's in the past now,' he sighed.

'The present madam. Nargis. What is she like?'

'Mm. Well, she is different. Less approachable. It's a bit like the reign of the Mughal kings over there in the Babur Chowk. The new leader kills the followers of the old regime. That's what happened after Sajida died. Do not repeat my words, I beg of you.'

'No, I won't.' Perhaps he's not in her pay after all, thought Karam.

'Her children disappeared: then she died.'

'She had a daughter?'

'Not by birth. She had sons. But Nur was her favourite amongst her adopted daughters. Very intelligent, college educated. Sajida was over-protective of her: that was probably her weakness. Nur was very musical, that was her value to them. The music became more popular than the dancing girls in her time. Even now you can hear her compositions over there.'

'Yes, I noticed the improvement last evening.'

'Well, the rumour-machine ran on overtime when it came to the selling of Nur's virginity.'

Karam winced, his head drooped. He hoped the proprietor hadn't noticed.

'Hundreds of thousands of rupees were being bid for her. No-one knows what happened. A date was set. Nur danced and sang for the highest bidders and disappeared that night. Some said Nur had been killed on her first night; by a rich sadist; by the greed of the new madam, for there was a power struggle, but who knows the truth? Sajida died and then we were all grief stricken,' he sighed. 'It's all in the past.'

Two customers arrived, the proprietor excused himself and Karam was left to finish his meal. He didn't feel like eating, his gaze returning every few minutes to his watch and then the entrance to the lane.

It was fifteen minutes past one, he'd wondered if she'd changed her mind, when a female figure dressed in a burkha with pink salwar showing under the hem appeared in the street in front of the lane. Men at the shops around stopped to look but, when she walked purposefully away they resumed their tasks. If she had stumbled or cried out they would have run to her side, Karam smiled at the thought. She crossed the busy street, skipping forward to avoid a rickshaw near the cafe.

'Hey, watch what you're doing,' she called after him and all eyes in the cafe turned towards her. She wiped down her burkha with a flourish, stood to give a Karam a look, and walked away. He wasn't the only man who rose from his seat, but he was the one who left money on the table.

'Goodbye, sir, see you tomorrow?' the proprietor called.

'Perhaps.' Karam walked into the street. Looking in the direction Jasmine had gone he saw a burkha-clad woman entering an Ambassador taxi-cab

'Oh well, I've lost her,' he thought, 'she's too quick for me.' He turned in the same direction, watching as the taxi disappeared around a bend. He thought the morning had been a waste. What would he do now?

The mosque was coming into view on his left hand side when a taxi passed him, stopping about twenty yards ahead. He kept his eye on it, a shopkeeper at the cloth store nearby also left his shop to approach the cab, thinking it was a shy lady customer, but Karam was nearer when the door opened to block his way. He held the door and looked in to see Jasmine's eyes, a nod from her and he was in the taxi as it drove away leaving a disappointed shopkeeper in the road.

She gave him a note, which said in beautiful Urdu script that she would leave the cab and return to it after about ten minutes, the driver knew where to go. Three minutes later she stepped down from the cab in front of a ladies tailors' shop. The cab drove on, circled the Chandni Chowk gardens and the Junter Munter Science Park, stopping at a well-known sweetmeat makers after half-an-hour. A burkha-clad woman came out, giving the cab-driver a note as she entered the taxi.

Karam watched Jasmine with admiration: if she had been followed, all these manoeuvres would have left the trail cold.

They drove towards Karol Bhag, the area where Karam had lived in his younger days and now he began to recognise some of the buildings. The gurdwara was no longer a square brick building but had acquired a white dome and marble verandas. The streets were as busy as they had ever been with many more cars, mostly Ambassadors made in India. They changed the sound of the streets from when he was young as the sound of their horns drowned out those of horses or oxen.

The taxi stopped alongside a modern tearoom, the kitchen at the rear, tables and chairs at the front behind a glass window and door. Across the road, behind a high brick wall with a gated entrance was a block of new apartments. Jasmine paid the taxi driver, whispering to Karam that he should go to the tearoom and with much swishing of cloak she left the cab. Karam stood in the street as the taxi moved away, and watched as

Jasmine approached the gatekeeper. She was obviously known to him for he acknowledged her with a nod and opened the gate.

Karam entered the tearoom, taking a seat at the window and ordering tea whilst keeping an eye on the gate and the verandas of the apartments above. This is a respectable area, he thought, and the woman knows what she's about. It occurred to him that he'd not heard her speak aloud. What a day this was turning out to be!

As he finished his tea, the gate of the apartments opened to let a boy of about fifteen, tall and slim with a topknot, the informal handkerchief-type covering that took the place of a turban, on his head. Karam thought of himself at that age, he'd joined the Congress party and had fallen for Takri; he smiled to think, at the age of this boy he'd believed there was not much more to know about the world. He watched the boy weaving through the traffic purposefully and entering the cafe. Karam looked around at the other customers, thinking the boy was coming in to see a friend, or perhaps he worked here. But the boy approached Karam with folded hands. Karam half-stood and waved a hand to the seat opposite.

'Sat siri akal ji,' the boy remained standing. 'I am Iqbal Singh. My... my mother wishes to speak with you. Umm, she is in our house across the road. Will you come... with me?'

'Sat siri akal son,' Karam was astounded on looking in the boy's face. It was as if his own younger self was meeting him. This boy had his eyes, his features and his height. He stared in amazement, forgetting to answer as tears sprung to his eyes.

'Sir .. Baba?'

'Yes... yes. I will come. I wasn't expecting... if you lead the way... I'll follow.'

228

The boy waited until Karam had placed a few coins on the table and gestured to the waiter. As he moved away the older man's foot caught in the leg of the table, making the boy leap forward to grip him by the arm. Karam thought how good it feels to have this lad help.

When they entered the gate the keeper gave them a bow, Karam followed Iqbal as he walked up one flight of stairs along the corridor to a door where the name 'Singh' was written on a white label. The door opened to reveal Jasmine, having discarded her burkha, looking pretty in light pink salwar-kameez with that mischievous smile.

'Come in,' her voice was melodic with a hint of fun.

She turned, leading them down the short corridor to a large room which looked towards the back of the building: a cherry tree stood resplendent in pink and white blossoms.

'This is my friend, Nur.' An arm stretched out towards the window where a tall woman, black hair tied in a bun at the nape of her neck, in a pale blue sari stood looking out at the tree.

The boy said, 'Please sit here, sir.'

But Karam could not sit down as the woman turned towards him. Yes, it was his sister all over again; a little taller and with his own green-flecked brown eyes.

'I've waited all my life for this moment,' she said, her expression grim, her eyes accusing.

Jasmine interrupted, 'I'll be going now. Otherwise they'll send a search party out.'

When Karam turned to look at her, she added, 'I told Nur about your visit to Nargis and how I listened at the window. She'll tell you more. I'm sure you'll have lots to talk about.'

'Thank you, Jasmine. You could easily have kept quiet. I would have left with nothing.'

229

'Well, I think you might not have given up so quickly,' she smiled.

She moved towards Nur, 'See you in a couple of days, Sis. That's if I can get away.' Nur nodded, giving the younger woman a hug. In the corridor Iqbal helped her with her burkha: the door closed behind her. He returned to the room where the man and his mother had not moved from their positions, he in the centre of the room and she at the window.

'Ma, I'll be in my room. I've got work to do for school.'

She nodded and was reminded of her role as hostess of the house: she gestured to Karam that he should sit. He lowered himself into a cushioned wooden chair: she took the seat opposite him with a small low coffee table between them.

'How did you find out about me?' she asked and met Karam's eyes with her own.

'From your mother. Did you know anything about us?'

'Only that my father was Sikh and a member of the Congress Party. My mother, Sajida, told me before she died.'

'Your mother, Sajida, was beautiful and good.'

'She's the reason I'm here, and with my son.'

'I'm sorry I couldn't see her again.'

'When did you meet her last?'

'About twenty-five years ago. I didn't know then that I had a daughter. If only... let me explain, I saw Sajida dance and heard her sing, nothing more.'

'Now that you know about me. What happens?'

Karam leaned forward, 'I needed to know what life was like for you. You seem well settled and I'm delighted to see that. I can tell your mother, ... your birth mother, that you're alive and well.'

'Do you think that's the end of it?'

'Only if that's what you want. What do you want, Nur? I'll do anything that's in my power.'

'My name is Nuraina. My mother, Sajida, changed it before she died.' She gave a sigh, as if a sad memory had clouded her mind, before continuing, 'Where do you live?'

'Officially, my home is in Scotland. In India I have land in Mehatpur which my nephews were hoping to inherit, but now ...'

'You're joking. You can't acknowledge my existence.'

'Of course I can, and I will. And Iqbal's. If you go to Mehatpur, you'll be recognised as my family without any official papers. You have cousins in the Punjab who look like you. I've been missing from there since 1919: it's only three weeks since my return. They don't know where I've lived, and can only guess that it must be abroad, because of the clothes I wear. But, I'm not putting pressure on you Nur. I only want to be able to see you sometimes. You're my only child who I was told about a week ago. The most wonderful thing is to see you sitting in front of me. And that is thanks to Jasmine. If she'd been out when I went to see Nargis, I wouldn't have found you.'

'That's right,' Nur looked away to the window: remained silent for a few minutes, as if putting away memories. 'My pupils will be coming soon, for tuition. You see, I teach music at home to supplement my income from the school.'

'Of course, I understand, you are busy. May I see you tomorrow ... Nur ... Nuraina?'

She continued as a memory seemed to surface in her mind, 'Most of the dancing girls were without fathers, we all dreamed of a meeting. I didn't think ours would be so controlled, so careful,' she shivered, clutched her sari around her shoulders,

231

tears came to her eyes. 'I used to pray that you... would come... and take me out of there.'

Karam stood up, as the rain battered on the window: he took his daughter in his arms and kissed her forehead.

'But you didn't...' she leaned her head on his shoulder, beating her fist on the other one, crying openly now.

'I'm here: so sorry I didn't know before,' he held her as she sobbed his own tears falling on her head. 'Don't cry. You've done so well. I expected the worst, a bitter, angry woman but you are strong. Thank God for that.'

The door bell rang. Iqbal came out of his room. Nur stepped away, gesturing towards Karam, 'Iqbal, this is your grandfather.'

'Yes, I know Ma. Aunty Jasmine told me before I went down to the tearoom to bring Baba upstairs,' he grinned and nodded at Karam. 'That's Rani, here for her sitar lesson, Ma.'

Karam said, 'I must go now. Could Iqbal come with me to my hotel? Then you'll know where I'm living.'

'Yes. Do that and open the door for Rani, Iqbal.'

As he left Karam asked his daughter, 'May I return tomorrow? It's Sunday.'

Yes, in the morning. Come for breakfast, please.'

Karam left Delhi six months later to return to Glasgow with Iqbal, who began a university course in Edinburgh. Nuraina had insisted that the past was a closed book, and they should look forward.

CHAPTER SEVEN

Baba Kam and My Grandmother Takri

I was seven the year Baba Kam returned from India with Iqbal, who then went straight to Edinburgh University with only occasional visits in the holidays.

Baba Kam and Betty rented a flat downstairs from Papaji and that was where he was in the October of my second year at high school when Bibiji, my younger brother Ranjit and I began preparations to leave for India on a school ship, the Devonia, that had been sold to a buyer in Bombay. It was a one-way trip with mostly Indian and Pakistani passengers who were taking advantage of the cheap tickets. Perhaps my parents discussed whether I should go to India, because Jaspal was to remain in Glasgow since he was now working as an apprentice. I only knew I was expected to go, I had no choice.

'Do you know you'll be getting married over there?' Baba Kam said to me.

'No, that's not why we're going. It's a visit to the family.'

'They'll find someone for you to marry.'

'I'm too young. It won't happen, Baba.'

'You'll not be too young in India. I hope you won't be disappointed with life there, Rupa. Good luck, my dear.'

My friends at school collected money to buy me a present. It was a crystal heart on a silver chain and a book of poems from Elisabeth who said, 'I bet the next time we see you, you'll have a dozen children.'

Even then I doubted that.

My mother wanted to return to show off her new wealth and to help her brothers financially. Nirmal and Ajit had fulfilled their ambition and now owned a business. Every year a calendar arrived from them, which was hung on our kitchen wall, proudly displaying, 'Basant Singh & Sons', the sign which was above their workshop.

We sailed from Liverpool, on the first of November, with passengers arriving to join the ship from all over Britain. The *Devonia* looked impressive on the dock with her newly painted white exterior. Papaji and Baba Kam came to see us off.

In the huge shed where we all queued until boarding time, I met Kiran, from the south side of Glasgow, who was travelling with her mother and younger siblings. Her aunt, her mother's sister, was also on the boat. Kiran's mother was pretty and always smiling whereas her aunt was often sour-faced. She kept tabs on my friend, criticising her much more than her mother did.

'That's because she's betrothed to the elder sister's son.' I heard my mother say to another woman. I was surprised to hear mention of my friend's marriage, because she was a year younger than I, although more mature and confident. I kept pushing the thought away that people could actually be thinking about me being married. Why did these adults keep saying these things? Grown-up people got married: we were still girls.

Kiran and I explored the ship together, and sometimes managed to slip away from our mothers to the bar, where there was a juke-box. It was such a delicious feeling, so daring to ignore the glances of men, and choose a song from the list. My friend had money because we did listen to the music.

The scariest night of the voyage was during a terrific thunderstorm in the Persian Gulf. We were lying on the deck because it was too hot to sleep in the dormitories, and in the bright flashes of lightning we could see flying fish swimming alongside the ship.

At Karachi, Kiran disembarked, and was immediately covered with a burkha; to me it was a cover to hide a beautiful, out-going girl: I remember being afraid of it. Kiran must be shocked to be under it, I thought. Why was it used? As we returned from shopping in the bazaars, I looked across the shed where they were waiting for customs clearance, and still could not believe that she was under that black cloth. She didn't wave. We exchanged letters for months, from West to East Punjab, until she was married to her cousin.

The voyage from Karachi to Bombay was short. We disembarked into a large shed where we waited with our fridge, cooker and hi-fi system, as well as three large trunks of clothes. I marvelled at how my mother managed to organise it all: she was six months pregnant. We were exhausted with the long wait through customs. At two o'clock in the morning we were finally given clearance, and I sleepily met my uncles who had come from the Punjab, one from my mother's side of the family and one from my father's. We drove to a cheap hotel through the streets of Bombay. I thought it shocking that people were sleeping on the pavements. The weather was warm, and sleeping in the open was no hardship, but these people looked as if they had no homes. I didn't know there were homeless people in all big cities.

Our hotel room was infested with ants and cockroaches. My brother and I sat on the string beds staring at the line of tiny insects and the high-legged gait of the roaches, having never seen so many insects in the same room. The toilets were communal and full of excrement: the smell unbearable.

Our uncles took us for lunch to a Punjabi restaurant. It was our first meal out anywhere, and it felt strange to be shown into a large curtained cubicle, which had a table surrounded by chairs. We tried to eat, but all the food was new to us, not like our mother's home cooking. Ranjit and I watched the adults eating and chatting: we couldn't understand their conversation but they seemed happy.

Life in the streets of Bombay was amazing. People walking or cycling, hundreds of them in streets wider than those in Glasgow. One woman, I remember clearly, stood out from the crowd, wearing a white, western style dress with a full, bouncy skirt and high heels, obviously hurrying along to work. Indian women in Glasgow didn't wear dresses, so it was a surprise to find a woman in Bombay doing so. In these dusty streets, I remember clearly how she stood out like a bright butterfly. She was my last glimpse of the west, a lost life as well as a lost voice for English had become my first language and the people around me couldn't speak it. I withdrew into myself only answering questions in monosyllables, if at all.

We endured the dirty hotel until the next day when our train was due to leave the Victoria Terminus for the Punjab. It was difficult to reconcile our negative experiences of Bombay with the wonderful site of the grand, gothic-style facade of this magnificent station. Although it was very busy we were in no danger of becoming lost, as our carriage was found for us, and my brother and I were soon seated. From the window of the train, we watched India unfold in front of our eyes, over the two days of the journey north. Tea and sweet vendors passed the window, and sometimes boarded the train, as well as beggars and train singers, and of course, passengers.

The clothes women wore changed, from long colourful skirts and saris in the south, to salwar kameez in the north. The men wore a lunghi, or dhoti, but in the north that changed to pyjama trousers. In the south turbans were utilitarian: a rough cloth wound loosely around the head to keep off the sun. Further north they were worn starched and expertly shaped.

The train from Bombay stopped at Ludhiana Station, and from there, we travelled to Goraya, a distance of about twelve miles in my uncles' Chevrolet car, an American import. They'd bought it second-hand, and no-one else I knew owned a car, even in Glasgow so I was impressed.

On the GT Road in Goraya my grandmother, Papaji's mother, met us at our ancestor Baba Rishi's Temple, where we paid our respects before going home. The car stopped between the ancient banyan tree and a huge red-brick arch, one of four that dated from the days when the village had been enclosed by a wall.

Walking through the Grand Gate, my brother and I marvelled at the long, covered, up-sloping arch that led to the brick-paved lane where the neighbours had turned out to greet us. It was evening, we were tired and afraid of these dark faces crowding us on both sides.

'Is this little Rupa? How she's grown!'

I looked from side to side at them, hating the attention from people who had obviously known me in the past, but I couldn't remember them.

The little square opened on the left: the well had been covered up and the ground bricked over. The door of my grandparents' house was at the corner of the little open space. The house was built of red brick with tiny windows high up, one storey with a parapet along the perimeter of the flat roof. The front door was of ornately decorated wood, with a short chain high up in the middle, which when clicked to a bolt on the frame could be padlocked for security. We didn't know it, but the brick floor in the house, the water pump and the electricity were newly installed for our arrival, with money my father had recently sent over from Scotland. We were amazed by the array of brass dishes and trays that my grandmother had displayed on a wooden unit in the main room, and we sat down on a bed in front of them and stared.

'Are they made of gold?' whispered Ranjit.

'I don't know,' was my answer, 'Papaji didn't say his mother owned gold dishes, so they can't be.'

Behind the main room were two stores, one for the wooden trunks, and one for dry wood and cow-dung patties, which my grandmother brought from the farm, carried in a basket on her head, for the cooking fire. The main room had two doors: one leading to a veranda, the other to an open area from where a stone staircase led to the roof. Under the stairs was a kitchen which had a fireplace with a hole to the roof where there was a square chimney-head in which bright green parakeets had made nests because the house had been empty during the days when my grandparents were at their farm. Our arrival disturbed the parent birds and as the tiny featherless baby parrots fell into the fireplace, my brother and I desperately tried to save them by carrying them back to their nests. However, it was a lost cause, the chicks died and the parent birds didn't return the next year.

A few days later, we visited Rurka and I remember arriving at the house to see, sitting on a low stool in the courtyard, my Grandfather Basant, his eyes half-closed, pink skin, white beard and eyebrows, like a thin Santa Claus with a round, white turban around his head. He wore a coarse white shirt with matching pyjama trousers and held a long walking stick.

My mother introduced me to him, motioning that I should sit beside him. She guided his hand, and he touched my face and head all over.

'Ah, Rupa, welcome back,' he laughed and hugged me, giving me a glowing feeling, like being loved from centuries past. He looked timeless, similar to the pictures of the Gurus on the calendar that was posted to us each year.

My brother and I were truly confused in this new place which everyone thought was home for us. It must have been a wrench for me when I left the village to go to Scotland but I had forgotten everyone. Scotland was my home now where my father, brother and Baba Kam lived.

The toilets and the insects made the place alien to us and we wanted to run away. But since our mother insisted that this was where we would stay, we had no choice. We were very unhappy for a long time, and if she envisaged a bigger picture, with a return to Glasgow, she didn't share it with us. We had to make the best of it. Ranjit started school while I was expected to learn housework and babysit my younger brother who was born in February. My understanding of Punjabi improved but my attempts at speaking were ridiculed.

I noticed that many houses along the Mansapuri lane were in ruins and I now know that this was due to Partition, to economics and red tape in the new India The Muslim families who had lived there had gone, though they were not forgotten for that was when I found out about Jenna. Her house was still called by her name. Her friends still grieved for her and in the absence of any news hoped to see her walk in to Takri's courtyard one day to tell them about life in Pakistan. In addition, Hindu and Sikh families had moved to Goraya, and other towns, to find work. Grandfather Basant's aunts and uncles had died, his cousins had all left, some to work in England.

'If your Grandfather had not become blind, we might have stayed in Delhi,' Grandmother Takri said as she turned her spinning wheel, 'Then this house could have become a ruin as well.'

'But we have always come back to the village. Look at me,' my mother said.

'You have returned and with so much, Saira,' said Grandmother. 'I wish I had achieved more in my life.'

'But you have, Grandmother,' I smiled and rushed to answer, as she seemed sad. 'You had us! We wouldn't be here, if it weren't for you.'

Everyone laughed at my broken Punjabi. I had only wanted to cheer her up, but later I wondered about the deeper meaning behind her words. What had my grandmother wanted to do?

'That's true,' she replied giving me a smile, but her eyes seemed far away. Quite often I would see her spinning, raising the cotton from the spindle up and down with her left arm, and turning the wheel with her right, but I knew her thoughts were in another place.

In Glasgow, I was unsure about boys, I would speak to them if they approached me, but I learned in India that there are more important things than being polite to a boy. In this way, the two societies in my life were opposites: in Glasgow girls actively pursued boys, in Goraya males were definitely predatory, whilst the females responded to their efforts with ridicule and anger.

I was amused at the reaction of the women at the Grand Gate lane to the young couple who rented one of the houses, of whom it was said disapprovingly and in whispers, 'Their marriage is a love match. tch tch. They met at college- girls are ruined by too much education.' I knew my mother agreed with them for she would often say, 'Why would you educate a girl. They're only going to have babies.' And so I was not sent to school as my brother was.

I now realise the young woman who was the talk of the village had achieved quite a feat in a society that encouraged segregation of the sexes in all spheres of life.

I heard that Nehru's government introduced many new laws to improve the lives of women - property, dowry and marriage laws. Many viewed these as a step forward, but in practice the new laws were disregarded. I was to hear of girls 'taking a share' of their inheritance from their brothers, as if it was wrong, and not their right under the law. The girls were afraid of being disowned by their families. I attended a wedding, which was the bridegroom's second marriage, and the first wife who still lived in the house, was there dressed in drab clothes, trying to keep out of the way. Although I sensed that the guests felt sorry for her, the wedding was not boycotted. At least, if anyone had not attended because of the blatant flouting of the law.

In August, following the monsoon rains, Grandfather Basant was suddenly taken ill. My mother went to Rurka for a day, and in the evening returned to Goraya to tell us that he had died of a heart attack. Two days after his funeral, we joined our mother in Rurka. There was still crying and wailing when new visitors arrived, and I was both frightened and mesmerized by the commotion.

My cousin said, 'Eleven days after Grandfather's death there'll be a party with lots of sweetmeats to eat and to share with all the families that we know, because he had been a grandfather of boys, and his family had prospered. That's the tradition.'

'Write a letter to your Papaji, and tell him what has happened,' my mother gave me an airmail form.

I could not have imagined what would happen after Papaji received the letter, but two weeks later we were in Goraya, cleaning up after our midday meal, when there was a rattle of the door-chain, and a clearing of a throat, that was a man's announcement of his arrival.

'Ah -hmm. Hello. Sat Siri Akal! Anyone here?'

I thought I knew the voice, but daren't guess, rising from my place at the cooking fire and peering into the veranda. There was Baba Kam, with his sparkling eyes and big smile, looking very summery in a short-sleeved shirt and white trousers.

'Baba Kam! You're here? It's so good to see you, Baba Kam,' I rushed forward to give him a hug.

'And you, Rupa. You're thin, aren't you eating?'

I looked away. It was a long story: the shock to my system that was India. Something to tell Baba another time: too sad for this happy reunion.

Later, over a cup of tea, he said to my mother, 'Saira, I am so sorry about your father.'

'It is sad, and I miss him, but he had lived his allotted lifespan. When I was young they were desperately poor, but they are wealthy now, and he was content.

'I decided to return after Jai told me Basant had passed away. You see, Betty has gone to Ireland to live in her uncles' house and I may go there too.'

When we were in our beds, one for each of us on the rooftop, Baba Kam and Bibiji talked quietly. I listened until I could no longer stay awake.

'There were some details of my life I changed in Glasgow, because I thought there might be complications if I told you the truth, Saira.'

'What were those, Chacha?' my mother asked.

'I knew your mother when she was a girl. We are from the same village.'

'Oh, Mehatpur? If I'd known I would have asked questions, and written to tell her. So, you didn't want that?'

'I was trying to forget, to hide. Do you know we were at Jallianwala in 1919?'

'Jallianwala Bhag? They lost my cousin and brother.'

'It was a very traumatic period of our lives. The children died, and I believed your parents blamed me. I blamed myself, and tried to disappear from their lives, from the Punjab.'

'Chacha ... you are Karam?'

'Yes, that's me, Saira. I am Karam Singh from Mehatpur. I knew your mother when she was a girl. That was a long time ago,' his voice faltered, and he sighed deeply.

'My father called you his friend.'

'We had a reunion when I was last here.'

He was quiet for a while and then continued, 'When you came to Glasgow; I knew you could only have been Takri and

243

Basant's daughter. And when I returned from my visit to India and meeting up with your parents, I still didn't tell you.'

'You're part of our family in Glasgow. Especially to Rupa who thinks you are her special grandfather. Why didn't you tell us, Chacha?'

'I like to keep things simple. Watching Rupa grow has been a privilege.'

'What are your plans now?'

'First, I want to convey my condolences to your mother.'

'Yes, of course. I'm sure that won't be a problem.'

'May I take Rupa with me?'

'Yes. She could do with your company. She hasn't settled here and misses Glasgow.'

'Send her back, Saira. She can return within two years, without new sponsorship papers, because she's a resident of Scotland. After that it will be more difficult, especially if she's married.'

I accompanied Baba Kam. The two of us walked up the lane, and stood at the open door. At the end of the courtyard near the door to the room my Grandmother Takri sat on a low stool with a piece of crochet in her hands. She half rose then fell back onto her low seat when she saw who it was. Tears flowed down her cheeks as she folded her hands in greeting. Baba's head was bowed making me feel this was a private meeting, and I shouldn't look on. The white sheet was spread in the corner facing the kitchen for visitors who wished to talk about my Grandfather Basant so Baba went to sit there cross-legged. Grandmother rose from her stool, sitting down at one edge of the sheet. I told my aunt that Baba had come from Glasgow: she sent for my uncle. Grandmother had pulled her scarf over her eyes to cover her tears. I sat close to her.

'What happened? Did he suffer much at the end?' Baba asked.

'He was fine in the morning, except he complained about a pain in his chest, but later when he collapsed we knew it was serious. By evening he was gone.'

Baba said, 'I remember the day he and I first met. Tirath Singh was with him.'

'Yes, they went to Delhi together,' said Grandmother.

My cousin came and motioned to me to join her: I went upstairs as Grandmother asked Baba when he'd arrived from abroad.

An hour later Baba and I left the house with my uncle walking through the village bazaar to the crossroads. He pointed out the workshop the two brothers ran, and the sign above, 'Basant Singh and Sons.' Baba told my uncle his father must have been very proud of his boys, and justly so.

Baba Kam came back to Goraya with me and stayed with us at the Grand Gate house for a few days then left to visit his nephews in Mehatpur. They worked on the family land.

One day Grandmother Takri sent my uncle to pick me up in the Chevrolet, surprising me with the news that I was to accompany her to Baba Kam's house in her home village with my cousin. Baba was so happy to see us, and I was delighted to see him.

After our greetings, he said to Grandmother, 'I passed by your father's house yesterday. You didn't inherit anything?'

'His cousin's grandchildren live in the house now and they are very kind to me, although I don't visit very often. My

245

father died before Nehru brought in the inheritance laws in favour of girls, so my sisters and I were given nothing. But we expected that.'

In the afternoon, we went to Baba Kam's fields, sat on a string bed near the oxen and watched them drawing the water. Each little can of water on the wheel fell over and poured its load into a channel that ran along the field of maize. It was a peaceful place. Baba wore a long cloth around him like a skirt, but he didn't look at all feminine. It suited him in the hot weather. My cousin and I played in the running water, and after letting it cool my hands, I sat down on the bank to dabble my feet. We saw another hut in the distance, and went to explore. Baba and Grandmother were talking about the past.

On our return Baba Kam said, 'Rupa, come and sit with me.' And we spoke in English.

'You've got lots to tell Grandmother,' I said.

'We're not getting any younger, so I'm talking as fast as I can to make up for the years we didn't see each other,' Baba's words made me laugh.

Then he became more serious, and taking my hand said, 'There's something I want you to remember Rupa, your Grandmother and I care about each other, and these years that have separated us don't seem so long, now that we're together. We don't want to be apart now. Do you understand?' Baba looked at me as if there was more to say, but he wasn't going to say it.

'Yes, I think I do.'

'In the future, if you don't see me for a long time, will you remember what I've said?'

'Yes, I'll remember.'

We looked towards Grandmother and my cousin who were throwing little sticks into the water.

'Your grandmother was married when she was younger than you, Rupa. You remind me of her.'

'Were you at the wedding, Baba?' I was pleased that he thought I was like Grandmother. Other people said I was too dark, too thin and too quiet.

'Yes, and I was very sad, but we were children, and not sure of our own emotions. Later, when we were grown up we knew we loved each other, but then we both had other commitments, other directions in our lives.'

'It's good that you're together again.'

'Be careful when you talk about us, Rupa. Not everyone will agree with you.'

'Baba, nobody talks to me here, anyway. They think I'm dumb. I can't speak Punjabi like the other girls, who ignore me. I want to go back to Scotland where I've got friends.' Tears welled up in my eyes.

'It won't always be hard. You'll learn so much while you're here, and your experiences in Scotland will help you too. Don't be afraid of the future, work hard and you'll find rewards.'

'Yes, Baba,' I wiped my eyes and tried to cheer up.

'Be brave, little one.' He hugged me, one of the few people who did when I was young.

We sat together watching the sunset over the fields, until it was time to go. The field worker came to take the oxen in to their stalls for the evening.

It was almost dark, when we made our way back to the village, spending the night with Grandmother Takri's relatives, then returning to our own homes. I continued to learn housework, sewing and cooking, as well as helping my mother to look after my baby brother. She needed me to do that for she began the building of a big house. I took Baba's words to heart, and began to settle down, to work hard in this difficult land.

CHAPTER EIGHT

Lost and Found

Two weeks after our visit, my uncle and Grandmother Takri took a trip to the Radha Soami religious centre at Beas, about forty miles from Rurka. It was festival time, and there were many pilgrims headed there, some walking and others on different forms of transport. There is always the danger of losing each other at these times, so that was why none of the children were with them. It should have been safe for adults, but it was on this trip that Grandmother Takri disappeared.

Afterwards my uncle came to the Grand Gate house to tell my other grandmother about it, and I sat with them. 'We had listened to the sermon, with about two thousand others. When we rose Chachi said she was going to the toilet, and I told her I would wait near the gate. When she didn't appear I walked all the way back to the ladies' toilets. I couldn't see her, and became confused and anxious because there were many women in white clothes. The volunteers who know their way about the complex helped me, but there was no sign of her in the crowds. The toilets are near the river and a woman showed me where the riverbank had collapsed, with the monsoon rains and recently under the weight of the crowd. She said some people had fallen in, and she introduced me to other searching relatives. By this time everyone who had come for the day's service had gone, and the place was much quieter. I sent a telegram home with the result that everyone who could leave their work came, joining the search the next day but finding nothing more.'

'Yes. That part I know because I came to look after Rupa and the boys, when Saira and Karam went to Beas,' said my other grandmother.

My mother, who by now had stopped crying, added, 'everyone has agreed that she must have fallen into the river and been swept away.' And that was the general verdict about my Grandmother Takri's passing.

Then, it was time for Baba to leave, 'I may not return to Scotland in the near future, Saira. I want to travel in Europe. To places I've always wanted to see. Who knows how much time I have left?'

'You know where we are, and you're in good health with many years ahead of you. When you've travelled enough, you're welcome to come and live with us.'

'That's very generous. Thank you.'

'Good-bye Baba Kam.' I felt so sad I could hardly speak. I wished I could go with him. I remember running into the back room and hiding behind the large wooden trunk before he left.

A year passed, and I continued learning housework, whilst my mother boldly defied her in-laws and built her dream house. I looked after my baby brother while she left the house with her face veiled until she got to the building site, behind my grandparent's farm, where she would supervise the work. They were affronted at her audacity, but her cousin was the master builder so they couldn't complain. When the house was finished, she decided that I should return to Glasgow within the required two years for a resident. She had also arranged my betrothal, without consulting me, which of course she wasn't required to

250

do, although she did place a photograph of my husband-to-be where I wouldn't miss it and I looked at it briefly. He was twenty and I thought him very old. Before I left, his family came to see me from their village which was about an hour's drive from us. I didn't speak to them, meeting only the women and children. His father and older brother were not allowed to see me, although I remember sneaking a look at them.

My uncle and I travelled to Delhi to the British Embassy to have my new passport stamped with an entry permit. I was interviewed by two white officials.

'What school did you go to?' one asked.

'I went to City Public Secondary,' I answered.

The other officer had a look at my school report card, and commented that I still spoke with a Scottish accent. I wondered if he noticed the look of gratitude and relief on my face when he gave me the entry permit. After that I let myself dream of returning to Glasgow, because during the last two years I'd completely blocked the possibility out of my mind.

I had left Liverpool on the first of November, and almost two years later, I flew out of Pallam Airport, Delhi to return to Scotland. An airline official met me at my transit stop at Frankfurt, taking me to where I could wait for the call for my flight. I thought there was lots of time, and must have dozed off on my seat.

Feeling a push, I woke up to hear the announcement, 'Last call for Flight L22. This is the last call for Flight L22 to Glasgow. All passengers should make their way to gate number one.' I was suddenly alert, and stood up to go, but in front of me, a few metres away, I thought I spotted someone I knew. I peered because I am short-sighted. I chided myself that it couldn't be

Grandmother Takri. What was I thinking? She had passed away, drowned in the River Beas over a year ago. But who had wakened me? I was sure I'd felt a push. Quickly, I picked up my bag and hurried to the gate. As my passport was being checked, I turned and again thought it was Grandmother Takri wearing a blue salwar-kameez, standing at the barrier, looking at me. And then - oh it was Baba Kam, moving to stand beside her in the checked tweed jacket he used to wear. I gave a little yell, and must have moved towards them, but the official tugged my sweater, gave me my passport and said, 'Be quick.'

I turned at the corridor, and looked back. Grandmother Takri, I was sure it was her, put up both her hands, in a blessing. Then, I saw two younger women, and beside them Iqbal, I knew Iqbal, it was certainly him. The taller woman smiled at me, and waved. It sounds silly, but I felt loved. I waved back, smiling. Baba Kam put his arm around Grandmother Takri's shoulders and his other arm around the tall younger woman. Were they his family? My Grandmother Takri and her daughter? I was puzzled and took a few steps down the corridor. No one was looking at me so I ran back for another look. There was no-one at the barrier. Had I imagined them? Was my head so full of stories, two years of talking to myself because no-one else would talk to me, and now my mind was playing tricks?

I remembered Baba Kam's voice saying that not everyone would understand, and I knew that this sighting of them must remain a secret. No-one would believe me anyway. But seeing them gave me such a boost. I lived my life aware that Baba Kam and Grandmother Takri were somewhere, thinking about me and I had to achieve as much as I could. For them.

The End of the Search?

And now, years later, I give the manuscript to my mother. She sits on her sofa and tries to read the beginning saying, 'Yes, I can work this out. Here are their names.'

She's pleased to see so much writing but I know she will not progress further than the first few pages. I suggest to her that Grandmother Takri might have had another child, one only Jenna knew about.

She says, 'they were extraordinarily close friends. But no, they couldn't have hidden a child. How would they have done such a thing?'

'What about Iqbal? If Baba Kam had no children, how did he have a grandson?'

'Oh, Iqbal was obviously his nephew's boy.'

'Baba Kam didn't say that,' I persist.

'No, he didn't. He kept many secrets. You're right about that.'

Grandfather Basant would surely have wanted us to know, and for me to find, not only Takri, but the men in her life. It has taken some time, and much growing in age and wisdom on my part, before I could piece together their story: the secret that was part of the lives of Takri, Karam and Basant, and the sacrifices they made. And now it's no longer a secret because you know it too.

THE END,

Acknowledgements

My thanks to Naresh Gahir who, years ago, told me, 'Go write.'

Thanks to the professionals who have helped me on this journey, Fiona Parrott, Alan McMunnigall, Geri Stewart, David Manderson, Zoe Wicomb and Irene Hossack.

To Leela Soma, and all members of Mairi Morton's Open University Forum, for years of writing friendship.

To my editor, Farhana Shaikh, who is brilliant, and for being patient with me, when I needed more time to decide on 'going public'.

To my loyal family and friends, who have waited so long for this book.

And last, but not at all least, to my friends Aileen Baird and Helen McLelland who, on reading earlier drafts, both said those magical words, 'I couldn't put it down.'

Palo Stickland

I was born in the Punjab, India and brought up in Glasgow where I have worked as a teacher and officer within the local education authority. From my studies in creative writing I have gained two post-graduate qualifications. Success in publication has been in anthologies in Scotland, and in winning The Asian Writer Poetry Competition twice. In 2012, my short story was published in *Five Degrees*. I am working on my second novel, *Moon River*.